YOGA POSES QUESTIONS

Kitty Kara

An environmentally friendly book.
Printed on-demand, with paper from an FSC-certified provider.

Also by Carole Kerton:

HOME FROM OM: THE LAST YOGA RETREAT
YOGA PRESCRIBED
*Both books are also available online from
Amazon, in paperback and Kindle versions*

WHY AM I HERE THIS TIME?
MEMOIRS OF A YOGA TEACHER

*Carole's informative blog can be read at:
https://yogaprescribed.wordpress.com*

YOGA POSES QUESTIONS

CAROLE KERTON

MARVELLOUS BOOKS

Published by

MARVELLOUS BOOKS
12 St Peter's Place BN7 1YP
info@marvellousbooks.com
www.marvellousbooks.com

First Edition 2017

Copyright © 2017 by Carole Kerton

All rights reserved. This book or any portion thereof may not be reproduced or used in any manner whatsoever without the express written permission of the publisher and copyright owner, except for the use of brief quotations in a book review or scholarly journal.

DISCLAIMER:

This is a work of fiction. Names, characters, businesses, places, events and incidents are either the products of the author's imagination or used in a fictitious manner. Any resemblance to actual persons, living or dead, or actual events is purely coincidental. Yoga is best practised in a class with a reputable teacher, as all yoga practices described need to be correctly taught. All suggestions enclosed are based on anecdotal evidence and yoga experience. They are in no way a substitute for medical advice.

ISBN: 978-1-909900-10-3

For all my friends – those to whom I'm related and those to whom I relate.

ॐ

Acknowledgements

Grateful thanks go to Tim, tireless, wise blog advisor,
And as well to Gemma, my loving sympathiser.
Cover lass, Liz, from *Yoga Prescribed*, lights up my life and my book,
While Amy, with her artist's eye, the photo for *Home from OM* she took.
Ben impresses and amazes, his cover shows his vim.
The look of *Yoga Poses Questions* is attributed to him.
From grandkids, I now express my thanks to husband, Mike.
He reads, corrects, listens, suggests, then goes out on his bike.
Even Rudi contributes, in his funny way,
With furry face and waggy tail he punctuates my day.
I wish to thank my can-do friend, Angela, and her flair.
With time and love she captured me and laid my essence bare.
Love to my dearest and close friends, all cheerleaders true.
They bolster me when I'm down and loyally love me through.
Cheers my weekly students, who deserve my appreciation.
They read, review, digest my books, add them to their collection.
And now thanks to a lovely lady, publisher Kristy Howell.
She works with diligence, patience (and with Rose) without a cross word or scowl.
Phew! The trilogy is now complete, *YP*, *HFO* and *YPQ*,
My final thanks, sincere, heartfelt, dear readers comes to you.

- PART ONE -

YOGA POSES QUESTIONS

CHAPTER 1

And Yoga asked:

"Why is it that people practise their yoga, attend the classes, understand the principles, yet they flee in the opposite direction the moment that a challenge occurs? I notice this particularly in reference to health problems."

Susie had been practising and teaching yoga for so long that yoga had become an entity in her life. She caught herself saying, "Yoga tells us" or "Yoga teaches us" in class, just as though Yoga was (and is) indeed a person, a best friend, a guide, the oracle.

This question came to her at the end of her early morning meditation. She had to admit it was something that had always puzzled her. She had students like this. They were sincere and regular, asked intelligent questions, practised some yoga every day, and yet the moment that they had a serious health issue they would turn immediately to conventional medicine.

"I'll give that question some particular attention, Yoga," Susie promised, as she plunged into her busy day.

As well as being a yoga teacher, Susie ran an old yogis' home with her husband Rob. Currently they had eleven residents, one of whom was Susie's mother. Running Home from OM was a challenge, but a most fulfilling venture. Each day Susie taught two classes in the lovely yoga hall, one in the morning and one in the late afternoon. The residents attended all of the classes, working with their own awareness and listening to their bodies. Susie insisted that the way to ensure folk were healthy in their later years was to keep them moving and motivated. Certainly her positivity and conviction created a healing atmosphere for her elderly yogis, and they loved her classes.

"Hi Joanna," Susie cheerily greeted her friend and colleague as she entered the kitchen of the home. "How are you today? Are you ready to spread love, light and cheer amongst our oldies?"

Susie's smile was infectious and Joanna grinned back at her. "Certainly I am," she replied, "and I've made them a pile of blueberry pancakes to start their day off with a treat."

Already there was a buzz of conversation in the dining room. The ageing yogis sat for silent meditation first thing in the morning, followed by a good yoga workout through all the joints. A relaxation at the end of the class allowed their minds, bodies and inner spirits to come into perfect balance. They definitely came to breakfast feeling refreshed and ready for a good natter!

"How are the newlyweds today?" Pam cheerfully enquired of Bernard and Valerie.

They looked at one another and grinned. "We're hardly newlyweds any more, Pam," Valerie laughed. "Rather we're an old married couple of nine months! But thank you kindly, we're fine. You see how established we are — I'm already answering for both of us!"

Bernard chuckled. "And how are you and Jimmy, Pam?" he said.

"We're fine, too," she responded immediately. "I reckon we'll all live forever, here in Home from OM!"

Maureen and Julia were tucking into the pancakes on the next table. "Now which of our *koshas* are we nourishing right now, Maureen?" Julia enquired with a twinkle. Susie had been teaching them about the five *koshas*, or 'sheaths', which make up the entire being. She had explained that we are made of many layers – much like an onion!

"Well," responded Maureen, "my physical body is definitely involved, my mind is gladdened by the anticipation, and these pancakes are heavenly — so that means I'm well on my way to bliss!"

Mealtimes in the home were always really good fun. They were a time for connecting with fellow yogis, a time to explore the philosophy in which they all believed, and a time to make plans for the day. Jamila, a resident and a yoga teacher, had been asked to teach a class for Elly, who was on a retreat. After breakfast, she made her way back to her room to plan her practice. Later, she would walk down the road to the yoga centre that Susie and Rob had created. When Susie's mother, Marion, had moved into Home from OM, she had left her house empty. It was the left-hand side of two semis, with Rob and Susie living in the other half. Susie immediately had the bright idea of turning it into a yoga centre. The downstairs became the yoga hall, while upstairs they created therapy rooms. Susie's wide community of yoga teachers and therapists had soon taken advantage of the facilities. The centre was thriving and proved a successful way to finance Marion's residency in the home.

Jamila was happily teaching Elly's class, while Susie was next door catching up on her chores. "I guess it is ingrained in folk's minds that a health issue must be addressed by the conventional medical route," she replied in her mind to Yoga. She was cleaning the bathrooms while she considered the question. "I feel that it's based on fear. Everyone is afraid of going against medical advice. But I do think that we're making in-roads. My students, whilst yes they do run straight to the doctor, they do also look for ways that yoga will support their treatment. I guess it just takes a very long time to turn the ship around. And I know what you're going to say, Yoga! You've been around for five thousand years! Well, all I can say is that I'm doing my best. Honestly I am!"

CHAPTER 2

And Yoga asked:

"Why do people forget their realisations? Why do they become distracted from the path so readily?"

Coming close on the heels of the first one, this question provoked an immediate response from Susie. "It's human nature, Yoga. Most of what we do in the practices is repetition. The human mind is wayward. It's like a butterfly, flitting from one thought to another. In the *Bhagavad Gita*, Krishna describes the mind as a chariot being pulled by wild horses! Many times my students tell me that their biggest challenge is quietening the mind. And until they learn to still the mind, absorbing the yogic teachings is haphazard at best."

Susie was taking the short walk to the home as she wanted to have a cup of herbal tea with her mother. She had news to impart. One of her sons, Max, had proposed to his girlfriend! Susie knew how excited Marion would be.

Susie found Marion in her bedroom. She was knitting baby clothes to give to the hospice shop. "Hi, Mum," Susie bent down to give her mother a kiss on the cheek. "Fancy a herbal tea and a natter?"

"Ooh yes," Marion immediately responded. "I'd love a fennel tea, please."

Susie popped along to the tea-station on the landing, and brought back two fennel teas. "I have big news!" she proclaimed excitedly. "Max has proposed to Megan and she has accepted!"

Marion's face broke open with the sunniest of smiles. "How absolutely delightful – that is big news!" she chirped. "Have they chosen the ring? When are they getting married? Was Megan surprised?"

"Slow down, Mum," Susie laughed. "Remember my boys keep details close to their chests! All I know is what I have shared with you. Max has proposed and Megan has accepted. That's going to have to satisfy us for a while but, I tell you what, we could go out later and buy congratulations cards."

"Good plan, sweetheart." Marion agreed. She couldn't stop grinning and she couldn't wait to tell everyone at lunchtime!

The rest of the old yogis were delighted with this news. They all knew and loved Susie's twin sons. Many of them brought to mind the pantomime that the twins had put on for them a while back.

"I expect Megan will wear a traditional long wedding dress," mused Valerie. "It will be a shame to cover up those gorgeous legs! Do you remember how lovely she was as Prince Charming?" There were murmurs of agreement around the lunch table.

The food at the yoga home was carefully selected. Joanna was their resident nutritionist and she realised how important diet was in keeping the elderly healthy. They all ate vegetarian food with a good emphasis on rainbow colours. Joanna had a chakra recipe book on which she relied. Balancing the energy wheels for the oldies was essential. Susie had impressed upon Joanna that it mattered that the food was prepared with the right energy, too. "Food cooked with love will nourish on a deeper level," Susie would insist.

Another aspect of communal eating which had proved particularly successful was the social element. There were three tables set up for the residents and they changed tables with each meal. This way they interacted with all members of the home, and conversation was lively. Some days it was news items that dominated their interchange, but other times it would be yoga talk. Sometimes a particular practice would set off an in-depth conversation. It was clear that today's main topic was the engagement between Max and Megan! How they all enjoyed the speculation about the proposal.

The home had also thoroughly enjoyed a romance which had taken place before their eyes: Bernard, a long-standing member of the home, had fallen in love with Valerie. They made an elegant couple, and their shared love had enriched the feelings of joy in the home.

Bernard suggested to his two fellow men, Jimmy and Miles, that they take a walking meditation. "It's a lovely day, guys, and I think it may be appropriate to leave the girls to talk weddings," he said with a twinkle.

That evening, Susie brought into the practise the question posed by Yoga. She asked her students to consider why repetition was essential in the classes. She asked them to consider why the human mind was so easily distracted. She gave them a mantra to work with in the meditation. 'Man' means mind, and 'tra' means tool, so a mantra is a tool to help the mind focus. Susie chose an old favourite: *OM Mani Padme Hum*, which can be translated as 'the jewel in the heart of the lotus'. Silent repetition of this mantra allowed the minds to become focussed and quiet.

On the way from the yoga hall at the end of the practice, Rosie caught up with Susie. "It's so interesting that you would ask that question today, Susie," she began. "I was considering the same thing myself. I've been with you for years and I know that I have made real strides with my yoga, but if I never slipped, never needed to be reminded, and never got distracted, just think how much further along the path I would be!"

"This is so true, Rosie. But we live in the real world, even though it's a gentle world here in the yoga home. We're human beings. If we were perfect, we wouldn't have any more lessons to learn here on Earth. We would make the move to Spirit World, having completed this incarnation." Susie looked thoughtful.

"Mm, I see your point. All will happen in the right time frame and, I suppose, we can try too hard. I wonder if our guardian angels and spirit guides ever get frustrated with us!" Rosie grinned as she expressed this thought.

"I don't think so. I believe they are endlessly patient. But I do know that Yoga occasionally questions why we cannot make the effort to stay more focussed!" Susie gave Rosie a quick hug as they parted.

Walking home, a little later, Susie remembered this conversation. She had noticed in the past that a subject to be considered would come to her from several directions at once. Sometimes these subjects were trivial, sometimes they were life-changing. She felt that when a message needed to get through to mankind, Spirit World would think, "Give it to the yoga teachers. They'll process it and pass it on."

She spoke to Yoga, in her mind. "I guess the answer to your question, Yoga, is that we're not perfect. It's the old 'three steps forward and four steps back'. Even here in the home, where we live the yoga way of life, we are still distracted by the everyday. Maybe our lesson, while we are here, is about dealing with our imperfections. We've come from perfection, where we knew and understood a clear mind, and a heart filled with unconditional love. That was bliss, but I'm feeling that here we must learn to accept and embrace our imperfections."

Satisfied for the time being with her conclusion, Susie continued with her day. She knew that another question would soon come her way!

CHAPTER 3

And Yoga asked:

"How can I help the world, right now, right here?"

Susie was teaching her weekly Wednesday class in the yoga centre when this query came in. She had taught this group for many years, but had recently moved them to the centre. She immediately threw this question out to her students, dispatching her planned meditation and asking them to consider this instead. She knew how she felt about answering this question, but enjoyed the time to consider if Yoga could indeed do more to help the world.

Three people lingered after the class to discuss Yoga's question further. Mary said, "When I tell other people that I practise yoga, I receive a variety of reactions. Most people immediately think of the fitness benefit. They imagine it's a form of 'keep fit'. Then some find it amusing and begin to say 'OM'. It's only when I meet another sincere yogi that I can have a decent conversation about it."

"Yes," agreed Janice, "but there are more and more people practising genuine yoga now. Everyone you speak to knows someone who goes to a class. Yoga has already done so much to help the world."

John nodded his head. "And, at long last, more men are practising it," he said.

"I suppose there is a degree of frustration in the fact that Yoga's message dribbles out, rather than setting the world on fire," Susie mused, "but what more can Yoga do to help? I think Yoga's message needs to be continually relayed, constantly and steadfastly. I think the question really is: 'What can we do as yogis, right now, to help the world?'"

"Yes," agreed John quickly. "It's all about the standing firm, isn't it? And, I think, taking opportunities to spread the word. I find that friends occasionally mention health issues or life challenges to me, and then I suggest that yoga might help. Some look at me sceptically, but others are more open. I don't need much encouragement to extol the virtues of yoga practice!"

"You're a top man, John!" Susie laughed. "A yoga teacher I knew many years ago used to say: 'Do your best and leave the rest'. Yoga is doing its very best, and we must do the same. We need to spread the word and live the life. As you say, let's stand firm."

When everyone had left the hall, Susie looked around gratefully. She fully appreciated how lucky she was. She had two beautiful yoga halls – one in Home from OM and one here in the building next to her house. This centre had been her mother's home, but now Marion lived happily up the road with the old yogis. Susie had broached the idea of turning this into a yoga and therapy centre soon after her mother moved. Her husband, Rob, and Marion had fully supported the notion, but where would the money come from for the necessary alterations? Susie, as was her practice, put this out to the universe. The answer came from a very surprising quarter.

Susie's mind returned to memories of her father from when she was a child. She had been extraordinarily close to Jim, and he had absolutely adored her. So many happy memories of playing in the garden with her dad, going on holiday in the summer and riding their bikes came flooding back. She had felt so secure in his love. One particular day sprang to mind. They had all been on holiday in Dorset. It was a glorious, sunny day with just a light wind. They spent the day at Knoll Beach, making sandcastles, running in and out of the sea and filling up buckets for the moat. Susie had collected seashells; she particularly liked the small, lilac-coloured ones. Marion had brought a picnic, and Susie remembered eating egg and mayonnaise sandwiches and carrot sticks. They seemed to laugh all day.

Susie locked up the yoga centre and popped next door for her lunch. Rob was working from home, so she moved quietly around the kitchen. Her dad had never seen Susie become a successful yoga teacher. Sadly, he had never seen her become a mother either. Susie often mused about how he would have loved her sons. Jim had left. He did so abruptly and permanently. They never knew what life he had led after leaving them, but Susie had managed to contact Jim in her meditation. She always felt that he still loved her, despite their separation.

Susie's mind returned to the day, not so very long ago, when she had opened her front door and found an envelope on the mat. The writing on the address was undoubtedly her father's. Two thoughts immediately flew into her mind:

Was he coming back? How had he found her? She stood, shocked and pale, and steadied her breath before opening the letter. She learned in the first line that, no, he was not coming back.

"If you are reading this letter, dear Susie, then I will have died. I have carried you in my heart all these years. You are my beloved daughter and I wish you nothing but the very best. I've done a little bit of detective work online. It seems that you have done well. I always knew that you were a gift to the world! In your little corner, you are helping our troubled planet. Bless you! And bless your family. I have instructed my solicitor to sort out my finances at the end of my life. He will then dispatch a cheque to you, along with this letter. I hope that the money will help with your mission and that my love will somehow, through this gift, lodge in the walls of your yoga establishment. Please simply say 'sorry' to your mother for me. I am a different person now from the husband that ran out on her. I wish her well. And you, my dear girl, I will meet again one day. Be happy. This comes with all my love, Dad xxx."

Susie had sunk to the floor after reading this letter. She sat there for several minutes absorbing the news. Her first thought was to say her blessing: "God bless his dear sweet soul and please free his spirit." She wished to commend him to Spirit World, and to send him on his way wrapped in love. It was quite a while before Susie glanced at the cheque, and when she did she was amazed at the figure written on it. Clearly Jim had saved well. This money would take care of the alterations needed next door; it would create her yoga centre. Susie was determined to have a plaque on the wall to celebrate her father's generous gift, and this immediately made her feel better. Her father's contribution would be a positive memorial to him. "Gosh," she thought, "my wonderful mother has donated her house to become my yoga centre, and now my father has donated the money to achieve the alterations! Thank you so much, universe!"

Rob and Susie had used the same local builder who had created Home from OM. He was a good man, a craftsman, and had become familiar with the yoga requirements. He did them proud. The yoga establishment was simply called the 'Yoga and Therapy Centre', but Susie kept the thought at the back of her mind that, one day, she might come up with a more inspired name!

Sipping her hot blackstrap molasses drink, Susie returned in her mind to Yoga's recent query. "Well, Yoga, you've already changed so many people's lives. Word is spreading. Right here we have two yoga halls where folk come and absorb your teachings. I would say, if you wish to do yet more for the world, please spread your light far and wide. Send the light to all the troubled areas of our planet. Yoga practice is supporting many different nationalities, many different abilities, and many different age groups. Use us. Use all the yoga teachers and all the yoga students to bring peace and harmony. Meanwhile, keep the questions coming! I'm listening!"

CHAPTER 4

And Yoga said:

"Why are there still teachers who do not teach meditation? After all, it is the cornerstone of yoga practice."

The old yogis in Home from OM loved the early morning meditation. Many of them still meditated on the weekend, when there were no formal classes. The home boasted a really lovely meditation hut in the garden. All of the residents were encouraged to get involved with whichever part of the home they wished and Jamila particularly enjoyed gardening. She kept the area around the meditation hall colourful all the year around, planting up pots of geraniums in the summer, and then winter pansies in the winter months. Working with the earth kept Jamila grounded, and put her in touch with her root chakra.

Rosie, on the other hand, was very knowledgeable about crystals. She had placed a large rose quartz crystal in the meditation hut. This, she knew, would fill the space with unconditional love. She had hung some crystals at the entrance to the hut, which sent out rainbows in all directions on a sunny day. Rosie and Jamila had discussed creating a chakra garden around the hut, too. Perhaps they could combine the rainbow-coloured plants with unusual stones, a Buddha statue and some herbs, which would add fragrance.

The early meditation was actually Bernard's favourite time of day. He was an accomplished yogi, adept at the asanas, and totally conversant with the ancient philosophies and texts. Bernard had spent a long time in an ashram in India. He had shared his love of the early morning sitting with his wife, Valerie. They were usually the first in the yoga hall, already looking serene when the others entered.

Susie opened up a discussion during breakfast. "Why do some yoga teachers not teach meditation, do you think, Bernard?"

"I have no idea," he readily replied. "To me it's what yoga's all about."

Jamila nodded. "I've always loved introducing my students to meditation," she began. "There are some who find it difficult, but we persist. At the very least, they are resting in stillness. This allows the nervous system to calm down, the breathing to settle, and the closed eyes to have a rest."

Valerie joined in: "I don't think I understood meditation at all until I came here," she admitted. "I probably looked all right, but I was using the quiet time to write lists and letters!" Everyone laughed!

Jimmy chuckled. "Bernard showed me the light a while back," he said. "I fidgeted my way through meditation until my dear friend here introduced me to walking meditation. That was a revelation to me. I finally got it. I would certainly not want to attend a yoga class where meditation was not present."

Everyone murmured in agreement. It was Julia who said: "Do you think it's fear on the part of the yoga teacher? I'm guessing that a newly qualified teacher might be anxious about putting her students off. And if the teacher is in it for the physical aspect, rather than considering the whole being, they might be simply more comfortable leaving the esoteric stuff out."

"You've hit the nail on the head there, Julia," Susie agreed. "You cannot beat confidence and experience. But the only way to get that experience is to throw yourself in at the deep end and just do it. My tutor would be horrified if anyone that she had trained omitted meditation from their practices!"

Maureen spoke up next. "If your first teacher includes meditation, you accept that this is the right way. I'm confused by these fusions that you read about now. You know the sort of thing? They combine, for instance, yoga and pilates or yoga and tai chi. That, it seems to me, is diluting both disciplines."

Jean, sitting to Maureen's right, agreed with her. "I think I must be a purist. Give me yoga practice with meditation in its rightful slot every day of the week!"

Susie left the group to continue their discussion. She carried dishes into the kitchen, as did her mother, Marion. "Mum, you don't have to do this anymore," she said.

"I know, dear," Marion replied, "but let's just say that it's my karma yoga. Besides, I wouldn't see my lovely friend Joanna if I didn't come into the kitchen now and then!" With that she gave Joanna a big hug.

Susie continued to consider the many different meditation experiences that she had encountered. She, like Jimmy, was a fan of walking meditation. Many years before, she had taken a yoga group to a wonderful centre in Spain. Each morning they climbed the quarter of a mile up the hill to the yoga platform. This they did in silence. It was a peaceful, harmonious and spiritual way to begin the day. It gave them an opportunity to commune with nature and feel the ground beneath their feet, whilst listening to the birdsong.

Susie remembered many occasions when chanting had taken her to a special place. Repeating a Sanskrit chant out loud with a group was a moving experience. The chant allows you to break through the everyday mind and to find the peace and stillness that lies beyond.

In her musings, Susie also brought to mind a session that she had loved during her training. Her tutor had introduced them all to mandalas. They began by colouring a mandala (a diagram used to aid meditation) and then they created their own. Quite recently in Home from OM, Pam and Julia had created a mandala from a fruit flan! Everyone had so enjoyed all the different colours and patterns. There were kiwis, mandarins and pears, which created a feast for the eyes and a feast for the tummies!

Joanna and Susie had shared meditations at a specific time. Although they were remote from one another, they were in tune and they soon discovered what support could be harnessed by working in partnership. It had brought them close.

Of course, Susie would be the first to admit that not all meditation experiences were pleasant! Some could be disturbing. Embracing the fact that yoga practice works with the entire being is part of the discipline. We're made up of two sides: the light and the dark, as the yin and yang symbol shows us.

The meditation during that evening's practice had a different dimension to it. Perhaps the old yogis were appreciative of this time of group quiet. Perhaps they were viewing it a little differently after their discussion. It occurred to Susie that perhaps Yoga himself was present in the hall with them. It felt as though his support came in behind them, to add weight and to underline the importance of *dhyana*: meditation.

"Wow!" Susie said to Rob that night as they prepared for bed. "The atmosphere in the hall tonight was extraordinary! It had been a good class, but the meditation took us to a different level all together!"

"I suppose," responded Rob, "that the longer you stay together as a group, the more powerful and profound your experiences will be."

"Yes, that's part of it, but I also know that there was a special presence. Would you think I was crazy if I told you that I view yoga as a person? To me Yoga is a being, neither female nor male in truth, although for the sake of convenience I refer to 'him'. I talk to him in my mind. He asks me questions and provokes internal discussion. I really feel his support in my life. Am I bonkers, Rob?"

"Well," he smiled that slow smile that she loved, "you've always been a bit bonkers! But no, I think it's fine to think of Yoga as one of the family. I guess you've rolled all your spirit guides, guardian angels and yoga teaching into one being. And let's face it – yoga is such a huge part of your life. Living the yoga way of life, as we do, demands a huge degree of openness to all means of expression. This works for you. But I might get a little concerned if you start laying an extra place at the table!"

This set them both off giggling, and Susie went to sleep in good spirits.

CHAPTER 5

And Yoga asked:

"How is it that a whole industry has grown up around yoga, such as yoga shoes, yoga socks, and even yoga holidays? Doesn't this distract from (rather than explain) yoga's eternal message?"

Susie did have to agree with Yoga on this point. She had been much amused to see yoga shoes advertised. After all, yoga is practised barefoot!

"I get the yoga holidays, Yoga," she replied in her mind. "That's a sort of modern version of the visit to the ashram. Many excellent teachers take groups away and give them a real, meaningful immersion into yoga at its purest. As for the marketing gimmicks that you mention, I suppose it could be argued that anything that encourages folk to embrace yoga practice is a good thing. I tend to feel that if people start yoga classes for the wrong reason, they may very well stay for the right reasons. That's the power and magic of the practice. But I do really see your point. We live in such a materialistic world. One of the aspects of yoga that

I have always loved is the fact that you only need you and your mat. Yes, we like to have a meditation stool and a lovely meditation shawl, but they're not essential. It's sad to see yoga become a money-spinner."

Susie glanced around her group that day in the Yoga and Therapy Centre. No-one there was ostentatious. Some of her students had thicker mats, which helped with tender backs or sore knees, but there was nothing glossy about their equipment. About once a year, Susie gave all her students a little talk on mat hygiene and how to wash and dry their mat. In Home from OM they washed all the mats twice a year. They take a long while to dry, so choosing the right time was important.

"How do you feel about the whole industry that has grown up around yoga practice?" Susie asked Miles as they sat in the lounge sharing a nettle tea. Miles was a very neat man, distinguished and contained. He had lived a full life running a successful restaurant with his flamboyant partner, Marco. Living in the yoga home was a total contrast to that life, but he loved it. He loved the yoga classes and the companionship of like-minded folk.

"To be honest, it amuses me," he replied, smiling. "It's just human nature, isn't it? Some people see the success of yoga as an opportunity. And for the most part it's pretty harmless. There will always be young trendies out there who will love to sport funky T-shirts. And there will be those who want to have their mat, shawl and clothes all matching. My concern would be that focusing on the merchandise might distract them from the message of yoga. I imagine that would be your thoughts too?"

"Yes," agreed Susie. "I'm inundated with emails trying to sell me equipment and courses. My delete button is well used, I can tell you! But as Jean said the other day, I'm in essence a purist. Helping people to understand that they can be healthier, happier and fulfilled by practising yoga – that is my mission. I just love to see a newbie increase their stamina, strength and suppleness. I love to see someone understand meditation and learn what relaxation really means. You can't become enlightened by buying socks, that's for sure!"

"I'm guessing that a lot of merchandise is bought as gifts," Miles suggested. "And that's rather nice. It shows support for a loved one's hobby or interest. I suppose it could be argued that it's the same for everything – whether it's golf, football, martial arts, or even handicrafts. An industry grows up around it all. Even churches can be very ornate, and they're very often supported by a shop!"

"That's true," Susie agreed with a grin. "It's the dilution which bothers me, I suppose. But then we live in the world, and yoga must be about the world. One thing is an absolute certainty: I will *not* be buying yoga shoes anytime soon!"

Susie continued on through her day. Her thoughts turned to magazines. There was one exceptionally good one which she ordered for the home. She decided to check how many adverts were contained in the next issue.

Keeping yoga pure and its message simple was definitely Susie's aim. Her commitment was total. She recognised how very fortunate she was that her husband and her mother embraced its beliefs, too. "I think that basically the real practice is winning, Yoga," she said. "I've considered carefully. Whilst my students are unlikely to remove themselves from the world and go to live in a cave in the Himalayas, I do believe that their heads are not turned by frivolous buys. We're keeping the faith to the best of our abilities in this tricky world of ours!"

CHAPTER 6

And Yoga asked:

"Bearing all that in mind, which of the classical yoga paths is most suited to this day and age?"

"That's a good one, Yoga," Susie said. "Off the cuff, I would say that hatha yoga fits our present time the best. This is the path that keeps the body fit, enables us to connect with the Supreme Being, and prepares us for *raja yoga*: meditation. But I'll 'think on', as they say!"

There were eleven residents in Home from OM[1]. There were two couples: Jimmy and Pam, and Bernard and Valerie. Then there was Miles, Maureen, Rosie, Jean, Jamila, Julia and Marion. They came from different backgrounds, were different ages and their abilities were various. What brought them together was a love of yoga. They had all, in their different ways, experienced the power of yoga practice.

---

[1] Their stories can be found detailed in the previous book of the *Yoga Prescribed* series, *Home from OM: The Last Yoga Retreat*.

"I loved that class, Susie!" Jamila enthused, as they left the hall one evening. "You know how, sometimes, you're right there! You're so focused that nothing could possibly disturb you. And then, when it comes to the meditation, you just melt into all that is. Your edges completely disappear, and then, quite suddenly, you can see the big picture. You know with every fibre of your being that all is well. All is going to plan."

Susie laughed. "I know exactly what you mean, Jamila. I'm so pleased. There was a special feeling in the room tonight."

"There certainly was," agreed Jamila. "Let me give you a hug. I feel so very grateful to have found you and to be living here in Home from OM."

This sort of feedback was music to Susie's ears. She so wanted the residents to continue along their spiritual paths. It was really important that she could go on giving them enough variety to keep them stimulated, and yet enough repetition to keep them feeling secure. This feedback was even more appreciated since it came from another yoga teacher.

The yoga practised in the home was hatha yoga, but this led them to raja yoga. Susie thought back to Yoga's question about why some teachers did not include meditation in their classes. Her tutor had instilled in her a belief that meditation was what yoga was all about. There are various myths around the practice of yoga, of course. Sometimes it is said that when the swamis and gurus came over to the West, to spread the word, they were amazed to discover that people could not sit still. So they designed a number of exercises and positions that would bring suppleness, strength and stamina to the physical body. Then, with better fitness, folk would be able to sit comfortably for long periods to meditate. However, drawings of the yoga postures have been discovered on cave walls and dated to five thousand years ago, so that does rather give the lie to the first story.

Susie went back to the Yoga and Therapy Centre to make sure that all was well. She had a friend using one of the therapy rooms for cranial osteopathy treatments that day. Susie was still working with the idea of setting up a weekly meditation group here in the centre. "I need three of me," she mused, not for the first time. "There are just not enough hours in the day for all that I would like to do!"

That weekend, Rob and Susie's son, Max, was coming for a visit. This would be the first time that they'd seen Max and Megan since they'd become engaged. Rob was cooking them all a special meal on the Saturday evening as a celebration. He was preparing a curry, a favourite meal for the whole family, and Susie needed to fit in getting to the shops to pick up the ingredients. "At least we don't have to think about Sunday lunch," she thought to herself. "Joanna's such a trooper to volunteer to cook for all of us. It'll be great for Megan and Max to see all the oldies, and particularly to spend time with Mum in her everyday setting. And the yogis are so excited to see the young people! Sunday will be a tonic for everyone."

This proved to be the case. All the residents of Home from OM dressed smartly for the occasion. They had clubbed together and bought a gift for the youngsters. Rosie presented this to them after dessert had been cleared away.

"We did some brainstorming," Rosie began, "and finally decided that the best gift for you both would be this. Every home needs one!"

The present was large and beautifully wrapped. Rosie struggled under its weight. Max and Megan wasted no time in opening it and were thrilled to discover that it was a statue of Ganesh.

"Wow!" exclaimed Max. "Now this is a clever gift! Ganesh is the remover of obstacles."

Megan was grinning mischievously, "And we've already discovered a few of those," she giggled. "Thank you all so very much."

The oldies were delighted that they'd got it just right, and Susie didn't know who she was most proud of – her son and his fiancée, or her elderly yogis!

Marion, meanwhile, had been working on a needlepoint for the young couple. It showed a beautiful building with a white picket fence, roses around the front door and a yellow Labrador sitting on the front lawn. It bore a striking resemblance to Home from OM, and, on closer inspection, there were two faces at one of the upstairs windows. "Now that is me with your dear old friend, Alice," Marion disclosed. "She was always so special to you two boys that I knew she would want to be part of this occasion."

"Oh Mum," Susie got up to give her mother a big hug. "How kind you are! What a very lovely thought."

Even Max's eyes looked a little damp at the mention of dear Alice. He had grown up with her living next door. He and his twin brother, Toby, loved nothing more than being invited to Alice and Ted's summerhouse for afternoon tea. Ted would tease them and tell them jokes, while Alice would ply them with scones, lemon drizzle cake and chocolate fancies. Ted and Alice had donated their home to Susie and Rob. It was their memorial really. It was a place where the elderly could grow old gracefully, in a loving and healing environment.

When the young couple finally left to drive back to London, Susie helped Joanna to clear up. "Thank you so much for that wonderful meal, sweetheart," she said. "You are such a good friend, and I do appreciate you."

"That's a pleasure," Joanna replied immediately. "It was my absolute privilege. I'm glad it went off so well. They're a gorgeous looking couple!"

"Oh, yes they are. Mind you, I am heavily biased," Susie admitted. "I hope that Toby will be equally blessed when he decides to settle down."

"We'll just load the dishwasher and then leave the rest for the morning," Joanna said. "Jane and I are planning a big clean up tomorrow, anyway."

Jane was the house manager, and a terrific asset. From her neat short haircut to her busy little feet, she was a paragon of efficiency!

Rob and Susie both counted their blessings that night. As Susie drifted off to sleep, she said to Yoga: "On reflection, I stand by my first take on your query. Living at a time when many people are sedentary, it's essential to find a way for them to keep their bodies fit. In addition to that, and judging by the loveliness of this occasion, I have to say that hatha yoga brings remarkable progress. Where would you find a nicer group of people? Where would you find more kindness, more love in any room? Yoga has given all these folk the gift of being themselves; the ability to tap into their inner joy. But hatha yoga, leading on to raja yoga and meditation, has also given them the wonderful desire to reach out to others. Thank you, Yoga."

CHAPTER 7

And Yoga asked:

"If hatha yoga best suits the times, why do people not take better care of their bodies? Even those who attend hatha yoga classes take no notice of correct diet."

"That's where living in a yoga community really helps, Yoga," Susie replied. "In Home from OM we research the most nutritious foods for our oldies. Their food is prepared with love, and we bear in mind the *gunas*: the three energies. We take care to give them some spicy food, which honours the *rajasic*, the get-up-and-go energy; some carbohydrate food, to honour the *tamasic* sleepy energy; but mostly we feed them *sattvic* food to keep them in good balance. They, for the most part, demonstrate the sattvic state of mind. So we know that it's working! But it's a different story with my weekly students. I do see how they neglect their bodies by being too busy to eat correctly."

Susie kept this conversation at the back of her mind that day. As she moved through the lounge to check that all was neat, she bent down to give the house cat a smooth. Kitty Kara responded cheerfully, purring and rubbing around Susie's legs. She was a dear little soul with an ability to seek out any resident who needed some extra love. Susie had noticed that she was hanging out with Rosie rather a lot at the moment. "I must check in with Rosie and make sure that all is well with her," Susie reminded herself.

Coming out into the garden, Susie spotted Jamila sitting on the garden seat and rubbing her left upper arm. "Are you all right, Jamila?" Susie enquired immediately.

"Basically I'm fine, thanks Susie," Jamila replied. "Yoga keeps us all so well! I just have an old injury in my left arm. It came about through helping one of my students. He was in the bow posture and I felt disposed to give him a helping hand. I went to lift him a little higher, but there was more resistance than I had anticipated! I gave the task a little more strength and felt the muscle in my upper arm complain. How many times do we say to our students: 'Don't force or push, always work with your body'? Well, clearly, I needed to learn that lesson again for myself! It's not a problem really. But it's just come to the top of my list. I've been designing my own self-massage and physiotherapy treatments."

"You're so wise, Jamila," Susie replied. "I'm a great believer in self-massage. Is it beginning to have a good effect?"

"Yes, I'm making slow progress. It seems to me that just focussing on an area brings healing. It's as though we have an inner caretaker who needs to be reminded about old injuries. I'm working with 'undoing'. I've established where all the sore spots are, and I'm getting my thumbs in more deeply. I reckon I've torn the ligament where it inserts into the shoulder. I suspect that it healed itself, but not completely. I shall persist!"

"Oh, that I know!" Susie laughed. "You are nothing if not persistent, Jamila!"

Susie decided to continue her rounds and to seek out Rosie. She tracked her down in her bedroom where she was reading. Sure enough, Kitty Kara was curled up on her lap. "How are you, Rosie?" Susie enquired.

"I'm fine thanks, Susie. Why do you ask?"

"Well, I'm taking my cue from Kara," Susie laughed. "That little cat is amazingly intuitive and I noticed that she's been spending a lot of time with you."

"Ah, do you know, my theory is this. I have a substantial lap – there's nothing bony about me! – so I've come to the conclusion that I'm the default person. If no-one is particularly needy at the moment, mine is the chosen lap for Kara."

Susie giggled. "Oh, that's lovely, Rosie! While we're chatting, though, I wanted to ask you how it was going with the volunteering at the theatre? Are you enjoying it?"

"Yes, actually, it's great fun. It was Jean's idea in the beginning, so we go together. We're usually required to put tickets into envelopes, but sometimes we get involved with the costumes. Last week we were recruited to paint some scenery! We always have a good laugh. It's such a splendid old theatre. Sometimes we're offered tickets at reduced rates or even for free."

"That sounds really lovely. I'm glad you and Jean have found something that you like to share. Well, I shall love you and leave you. Enjoy your book!"

Next Susie looked into the kitchen. She found Joanna and Jane discussing that week's menus.

"Hi lovely ladies," Susie began, "I've been reminded how important diet is in the practice of yoga. Do you ever run out of ideas?"

"Actually no," Joanna replied immediately. "This new chakra cookbook that I have is really inspiring."

"But," said Jane, "I was just saying to Joanna that I wished my daughter would be as thoughtful about her food choices. It seems that the first thing to hand will do as far as she's concerned. I worry for my little grandson. He's fed well when I'm there, but the rest of the time it's pretty random."

"I know what you mean, Jane," Susie replied. "I had this talk with my sons when they first left home. They'd been brought up as vegetarians and with well-balanced nutrition, but sometimes the very speed of life gets in the way of good choices."

"It's just planning really, isn't it?" suggested Joanna, "It's actually just as easy and quick to prepare nourishing food as it is to go to a shop or take-away place. I think the problem is that folk don't consider it to be a high priority."

"Yes, you're right," Susie agreed. "There's also this treat thing. People seem to believe that they 'deserve' a treat at the end of their working day. They believe that what constitutes a treat is 'naughty stuff'. I'm convinced that if they had a conversation with their bodies, the last thing the digestive system would ask for would be junk!"

"Well, no junk here," laughed Joanna. "I love that our oldies enjoy their meals. They're an advert for healthy vegetarianism!"

Susie planned to cover the first rule of yoga again in her classes. *Ahimsa* means non-violence and that is why yogis are vegetarian. You can't eat an animal without killing it first. It's been said that if abattoirs had glass walls, everyone would become vegetarian.

"I feel that we're making very slow progress on this one," Susie admitted to Yoga. "Old habits and ingrained beliefs feature in this discussion. There are still those who believe that a meal without meat is not a meal at all. They seem immune to the suffering of animals. Also, there is still that archaic attitude that humans are more important than animals; that somehow they don't matter. Even some of the yoga teachers I know still eat meat. I call them cosmetic teachers! Really they have not embraced the fundamentals of yoga philosophy. The fact is that if *they* have not embraced it, they're not teaching it to their students."

Susie was a yoga teacher who lived the yogic way of life. She didn't modify the beliefs for her own comfort, nor did she sugar-coat them for her students. She knew that being a vegetarian raised the energy vibration. Being kind to other creatures was essential, and spreading a high vibration out into the world was serving everyone – humans and animals.

CHAPTER 8

And Yoga asked:

"How can we convince people that the mind is not the boss?"

"This is another good one, Yoga," Susie replied in her mind. "This actually leads on from your last question, doesn't it? Once the mind is disciplined and understands its place in the team, it allows the body to dictate the diet that is best for the whole being."

Bernard had gathered a group together for a long walk. Several of the residents had been ramblers before becoming residents in Home from OM, so they were happy to take off for the day. "Bring sensible layers," Bernard had insisted, "the forecast has mentioned showers."

Bernard and Valerie led at the beginning. They had planned a route that would take them to a lovely little pub for lunch. One aspect of the group walk, which they all loved, was that they would quite naturally fall into twos and threes. They would chat happily and then, after a while, would find themselves walking along next to someone else.

In this way the time passed most pleasantly, and they always learned something new about one another.

Valerie was walking with Miles. "How's life then, Miles? Or, as my father used to say, 'What do you think of life in general?'"

"Well," replied Miles, "putting politics to one side, I feel quite upbeat about life in general. We're making progress on a lot of fronts, I think. Whilst social media definitely has its down sides, it has opened up the world and improved communication. And I do enjoy being in touch with friends across the world through Facebook."

"Yes, I agree with you. I guess, if I have concerns, it would be about the focus on the mind. Youngsters have become so absorbed with their devices that they are in danger of neglecting exercise." Valerie looked thoughtful.

"There should definitely be more yoga in schools," Miles proclaimed, firmly. "It would be so helpful for those children who are not interested in sports, but need to keep their bodies fit."

"Definitely," agreed Valerie, "and it's fun!"

"Life is so fast for the young. There are exam pressures, peer pressures, tension in families. It's not easy for them. I was talking to Susie about this once. She said that she won't be happy until there's a resident yoga teacher in every school!"

"Dear Susie," Valerie smiled. "She's a mover and shaker! What an example she is to the world. She literally lives her yoga, and her enthusiasm is completely infectious. I love to watch her move. She has such grace. You know that she is grounded, aware of her physical body, and not living in her mind, as so many people do."

Just at that moment, Miles and Valerie caught up with Bernard and Julia. "The pub is in sight," Bernard said. "Have we all worked up a good appetite?"

Meanwhile, the subject of Valerie's discourse was at that moment considering Yoga's question. She had students in her classes who were completely unaware physically. They did, literally, live in their heads. As much as she repeated the yoga instructions to 'listen to your body' and to 'work with your own awareness', it was clear to see that they were permanently distracted. Life seemed somehow to be designed to argue with yoga!

"Do you think humans come programmed nowadays, Yoga? Do they come already equipped to keep their minds busy? Are they trained on some level to resist quietness? Some of my students fill the quiet spaces of the class with hectic thoughts. You can observe them spring into action the second the practice finishes. They're out through that door and off into their frantic day and frantic life. In these cases, there's no convincing them that the mind is not the boss!" Susie considered the techniques that best helped her when her mind was overloaded. After so many years of yoga practice, it felt enough for her to just get out her mat!

Rob was drawn into this question as they sat and ate dinner together. "Who's the boss for you, Rob?" Susie queried.

"You are!" Rob replied immediately – diplomacy and humour taking over!

"I know that!" she laughed. "No, I mean, who's the boss in your inner team? When you think of your body, mind, emotions and inner spirit, which one is the dominant member of the team?"

"Ah," replied Rob, "It's a deeper question. Well, I've done enough yoga practice to understand how I should answer this question. I should say that all members of the team are equally important. However, to be totally honest, I must admit that my mind is the most challenging part to work with. It's demanding. One time you likened the mind to a three-year-old who was pulling at your trousers. And my mind is sometimes like that – demanding my attention and not taking 'no' for an answer. When I experience that situation, I very purposely come back to my body. If it's in meditation, I concentrate on my mudra. I observe the connection between the finger and the thumb. And I feel myself sitting on the mat; I check that I'm evenly spread over both buttocks; I check that my shoulders are dropped. So I do those sorts of checks, and my mind becomes involved in awareness again."

"Yes, that's the way. It's an endless challenge to quieten the mind, isn't it? Do you know what I've discovered? If I've been laughing with someone immediately before the practice, my mind is totally obliging! I believe that laughter relaxes the mind in a rather special way." Susie grinned at her husband.

"Well, maybe you need to instigate some laughter at the start of every practice," Rob ventured. "At least laughter is not a problem for us, is it? We've always shared the same daft sense of humour!"

"You're right. It's certainly part of the glue that keeps us together. I remember someone once saying that 'enlightenment does not have to be serious!' And whenever you see footage of the Dalai Lama he will be grinning or chortling. His face cheers you up immediately."

It was at 2.00am that morning that Susie's mind came up with something most useful. She sat up in bed and said, "WELLNESS WITHIN!" Rob, sleepily, gave her a friendly pat and fell back to sleep. "That's a great name for the Yoga and Therapy Centre," Susie thought to herself. "I love the ambiguity of it. Well done, mind. You're a great team member! Thank you." She drifted back to sleep, but the name 'Wellness Within' was her first thought on waking.

CHAPTER 9

And Yoga said:

"What about the dreamers, Susie?"

Susie had just settled her old yogis in relaxation. It was late afternoon and was becoming dusk. There was a mellow feeling in the yoga studio and a special light which gave the impression that all the shapes were soft and without edges. Susie was herself 'wide open' after the meditation.

"Oh, Yoga," she thought, "this resonates with me. I was such a dreamer and I can readily return to times in my childhood when the days were endless. When lying on my back to watch the clouds pass was not a waste of time but a joyful occupation. I remember playing pretend with my dad and my dolls. I would serve them all imaginary tea. My dad and I would make up stories. We would dream up these amazing plots and embellish them with colourful characters and exotic places. I still remember some of the names of the countries we invented – Singrosia, Manycatsland, and Northtobedfordshire." Susie's eyes misted over. She glanced around her class. Yes, there were dreamers here too.

A huge wave of sadness swept over the yoga teacher. She felt that she could see the reason for this question. Where had all the dreamers gone? Life was now so busy. The pace of life had become so frantic, so hectic. When was their time for dreaming?

Susie brought her yogis around from their relaxation. She bade them goodbye and made for home. She was teaching a class that evening in the yoga centre, but she badly needed some quiet time. She made for her big chair and sat with her eyes closed. The profound sadness was still with her. Tears rolled down her cheeks. She felt so sad that the world was too busy for dreamers, and she felt also that it was too harsh for dreamers. This notion was painful. Susie sat with the sadness and endeavoured to explore why this thought was so very raw.

Time passed. Susie would need to eat before she prepared for her next practice, yet she was not ready to move. This extreme despair that she felt for all the dreamers in the world was real and it needed to be acknowledged.

"Dreamers bring the magic to the everyday, Yoga", she breathed. "Dreamers create the beauty of the world. They're the artists, the musicians and the storytellers. It makes my heart ache to think that we're not allowing them the space and the time to dream. We're starving the world of the light and the delicate."

Susie wiped her eyes. "And what of the dreamer in all of us?" she continued. "What about that little entity, deep within, who still believes in 'happy ever after'? Who still believes in romance and eternal love? Who refuses to be realistic and practical?"

Life interrupted Susie's reverie. Food must be eaten. Yoga must be taught. This question from Yoga nagged at the edges of Susie's mind and she returned to it later. It fascinated her that she had been so moved. Would she describe herself as a dreamer? Yes, she definitely would. Did she make time for dreaming? No, she definitely didn't. She remembered thinking, quite recently, that she needed to be split into three. Her busy life claimed every ounce of her strength and every second of her time.

"Rob, I need to watch a weepy movie this weekend," Susie confided later. "I'm super emotional."

"That's fine, sweetheart," he replied. "How about if we watch that Cary Grant movie that you love? I mean the one where they planned to meet on top of the Empire State Building?"

"Yes, that would fit the bill," Susie agreed. "There's something about watching a sad movie that somehow allows you to have a good bawl! It seems fine to cry for the characters, but somewhat indulgent to cry for yourself! I love *An Affair to Remember.*"

"Anything you want to talk about?" Rob reached for his lovely wife's hand.

"No, thank you Rob, but it's very sweet of you to care. I need to mull this over a bit more. It's something that Yoga asked. It's pushed my buttons."

Rob gave Susie's hand a squeeze. He knew that she would talk when she was ready.

The next day, Susie made time for a walk. She often did her best thinking while walking. She had realised that her life was too busy for her to sit and dream. And she had realised that she missed that part of her that was the dreamer. She loved her life. She had truly created her own reality, with her husband's help. She loved that she was serving the community with her yoga classes and her old yogis' home. Indeed, Susie had manifested her dreams. But where were her dreams right now? Yoga had prompted her to look at the present, and she had seen that her life was so full, so busy, that dreaming had dropped off the end. She wasn't even 'dreaming up' projects for their home anymore.

Susie considered how many hours per week she spent teaching yoga. She loved every moment, of course, but yoga was a discipline. Yes, it was true that this very discipline offered incredible freedom, but was it too prescriptive? Susie felt uplifted and liberated by her practices, but perhaps there was not enough scope for creativity. As she walked, she took an overview of her life. She recognised the important truth that Yoga had brought to her attention. The world needed dreamers. She must bring 'dreaming' into her life once more. And, she felt, she must bring an element of dreaming into her yoga classes.

Watching the movie with Rob that weekend gave Susie permission to cry. The release was thorough and much needed, and she felt a good deal better afterwards. A plan was forming in her mind. She had retrieved her sketch book from the trunk on the landing and had begun to play around with some designs. She had planned in some visualisations for her classes, too. It was lovely to create pictures and to use guided imagery, which she had neglected for a while.

"Thank you for that question, Yoga," Susie said, in her head, at the end of the afternoon class. "It's so important to remember that the world needs dreamers. When we look back to the yogic philosophies, the important messages were conveyed by stories. Reading the *Gita* brings the teachings to life. The descriptions are rich and lyrical. Yoga teachers need to take time to dream, and I'm determined to make that time. In fact, I shall actively enjoy visiting the lovely corner of my mind where daydreams live."

CHAPTER 10

And Yoga asked:

> *"Why aren't there more medics, doctors, consultants – indeed all health professionals, spreading the word of yoga?"*

This question was less personal and Susie could address it analytically. "There *are* more enlightened health professionals extolling the virtues of yoga practice actually," Susie enthused. "I read an article just last week about a GP who prescribes yoga. He offers his patients a free taster class at the local yoga studio. But this is a good reminder. Our doctor is Indian and is really pro-yoga. He's written a remarkable paper on the subject of our old yogis' home, which I'm hopeful will encourage debate amongst the medical profession."

Indeed, Dr Iyer was visiting Home from OM that very day. He kept a close eye on Jimmy, after his episode with bowel cancer, but he also wanted to check on Jean. She had developed a perpetual and irritating cough.

"Good morning, Susie," Dr Iyer said. Jane had answered the door to him and taken his coat. "This rain is persistent.

How fortunate your oldies are that they don't have to go out for their yoga practice!"

"That's true," Susie agreed. "The only one put out by this downpour is the cat!"

Susie and the doctor chatted companionably as she walked him to Jean's room. There she left the two of them for the consultation.

Susie popped her head around her mother's door, while she was upstairs.

"How are you today, Mum?" she said, smiling brightly.

"I'm well thank you, Susie," Marion replied. "And how are all of you? Any more news about Max's and Megan's wedding?"

"No, we've heard nothing concrete. I'm hoping that they'll pop down again soon and update us. I'm assuming that Toby will be best man!"

"Oh, of course he will be! Max wouldn't consider anyone other than his twin! How is Toby?" Marion patted the chair next to the window and Susie sat down. Marion perched on the end of her bed.

"To be perfectly honest I'm a little concerned about him, Mum."

"Why, what's going on? He's happy with his job, isn't he?" Marion looked concerned. She adored her grandsons.

"Yes, work is going really well. He's found his niche there, but I have a hunch that things aren't rosy with Jasmine. It's more what he's not saying, than what he is saying, if you know what I mean." Susie frowned.

"Mm," Marion replied. "Toby always went quiet when dealing with an emotional problem. Don't worry, my love, he's like you. He'll open up when he's ready."

"I'm sure you're right, Mum," Susie agreed. "It's harder for young men to express their emotions, somehow. I'm guessing that he doesn't want to bother Max right at the minute. He won't want to put a damper on his happiness. I'm going to put him in the healing book – that won't hurt, and it may help."

Meanwhile, Dr Iyer was satisfied that Jean's cough was the result of a virus and would clear in time. She had assured him that she was drinking lemon and honey hot drinks, and that she was gargling with cider vinegar in lukewarm water. He was amused to note that she had a cut onion beside her bed! This was one recommendation of Susie's which he and his family had adopted. She was adamant that the onion absorbed the germs.

"I was reminded today, Dr Iyer," Susie began, "that we need to keep up the pressure on the medical establishment. Do you think more health professionals are embracing the benefits of yoga practice?"

"Yes I do, Susie," he replied immediately. "There are still those who are 'old school' and resistant, but the evidence increases every day. My paper about your home was well-received. One of the biggest problems for the Health Service right now is the number of old folk in the country, and how we support their health needs. I was talking to a friend of mine who is a hospital consultant. He says they have two massive headaches. One is there are not enough beds available in the Intensive Care Unit. Having no after-care means that operations cannot take place. There's a huge backlog in the system. Every time an operation is cancelled, that delay ripples right down through the hospital. So many people are being disappointed. The second headache is getting old folk off the wards and into rehabilitation establishments. Beds that should be available are not because these patients have nowhere to go. So, of course, these two problems are connected. The best solution to both difficulties is to keep the old folk healthy!"

"I say 'Amen' to that!" Susie responded. "This is relevant to me on two levels: firstly, because my mother is getting older, and secondly because my mission is to keep all my old yogis well and happy. Thank you for all your support, Dr Iyer."

"That's a pleasure, and you keep up the good work. Something has just occurred to me, Susie. Would you be prepared to give a talk to some of my colleagues? We've got a day's meeting coming up. Basically it's to discuss improvements in our practice, but you could really give them food for thought."

"I admit that the idea makes me feel a little nervous," Susie said, tentatively, "but, yes, I'm up for it. Let me know the date and the time."

Dr Iyer donned his substantial raincoat and went on his way. He left Susie wondering when she would find the time to write her talk, but she knew that this was important work. "There, Yoga, an opportunity to spread the word amongst the medical fraternity has appeared. Did you have anything to do with that, I wonder?"

Thoughts of writing her talk soon disappeared. It was Julia's birthday and her daughter, Laura, had taken her to the theatre. They came back full of the experience, but soggy around the edges. Susie knew that Joanna and Jane had baked a surprise cake for after dinner. One of the skills that Jane had brought to her job as house manager was a nifty way with icing. This particular cake was a triumph, proudly displaying a large 'OM'. It was devoured with gusto after the evening meal, and everyone proceeded to the lounge to chat and to present Julia with her gift. They had clubbed together and bought two pairs of bamboo yoga trousers. One pair was warm and quite heavy, perfect for the winter, and the other pair was light, perfect for the summer. Julia was delighted!

CHAPTER 11

And Yoga asked:

"Which chakra needs to be opened and stimulated in humans in general? Where can we focus to achieve our ends of spreading the word amongst the population and the medical establishment?"

Susie placed a heavy emphasis on work with the chakras: the wheels of energy. She regularly recited the seed sounds, which she found enormously helpful. It was a sort of first aid for the energy sheath! Her first instinct was to reply, "The heart chakra, Yoga. We need more love, more compassion, more gratitude in the world," but she would give some more consideration to this weighty query.

Rob had ordered a plaque for the Yoga and Health Centre. 'Wellness Within' was such a clever name that he wanted to do it justice. He chose a beautiful wooden sign, that was highly polished, and he added a strip of coloured glass to the right-hand side. The glass displayed red at the bottom and moved up through the chakra colours to violet at the top. He had planned it as a surprise, but Susie got to it first. She happened to be at the front door when the postman delivered the package, and was immediately intrigued. She could not have been more delighted with the finished article. Her text to Rob was effusive: "So thrilled with the plaque! Thank you so much. Can't wait for you to put it on the wall! Xxx"

All the therapists and yoga teachers who used the premises were delighted too, despite the fact that they would have to print new leaflets to incorporate the change of name. The village was beginning to be known as the 'yoga village', which amused Susie no end.

Friday evening brought another surprise for Susie. Toby arrived home unexpectedly. His parents, whilst thrilled to see him, immediately realised that all was not well. They both gave him big hugs, and shepherded him into the lounge. Toby glanced around appreciatively. He loved this house, and what he needed most of all was to feel embraced by it. He craved the unconditional love that only his parents could supply.

With a cup of tea in his hand, Toby broached the subject that was bothering him. "Well, you've obviously both guessed that something is awry, so I may as well disclose all." Susie and Rob looked lovingly at their son, and murmured words of encouragement. "It's all about Jas and me, actually. We've been on a slow decline. I guess it's fair to say that the writing has been on the wall for a while. She's been spending a lot of time out. She prefers to be out with her friends, getting drunk, than home with me. There are faults on both sides, of course. I have to admit that I've been neglecting her. Work's been really busy and I've needed time out on my bike to clear my mind. But I knew we were heading down the path of no return. What really brought it home to me was the last time I saw Max and Megan together. They're just so in tune! I'm really happy for Max, but it just proved to me what I already know and was trying to ignore. Jasmine and I haven't got a forever relationship, I'm afraid." Toby rubbed his forehead in a gesture that pulled on Susie's heart strings. She remembered him doing just that when he was bewildered as a little one.

"So, what happened, Toby?" Rob prompted.

"Well, it all came to a head last week. I came home late from work, the flat was in a mess and I could tell, by the clothes liberally spread all over the bed, that Jas had gone out clubbing again. I just didn't have the energy to start tidying up, so I resorted to the old favourite of beans on toast and collapsed in front of the television. I promptly fell asleep there, and I didn't wake until Jas fell in through the front door at 3.00am. She looked awful, and you know how you can suddenly look at someone and think, 'This is a stranger – I don't know this person any more'? Well, in all fairness to her, I did wake up cross with a crick in my neck, but I just knew in that second that we were all over." Toby looked weary.

"How did she take it, my love?" Susie enquired.

"I must have looked pretty cold," Toby admitted, "and I was quite clinical. I just said, 'This isn't working anymore, Jasmine. Our relationship is over. I shall leave for work in the morning, then I'll kip over with a friend until the weekend. I want you gone by the time I come home on Sunday evening.' She'd obviously put away a fair amount of alcohol, so her reactions were slow. I think basically she was astonished that the nice guy suddenly turned. She thought that I would put up with anything that she wanted to dish out. She slammed into the bedroom. I slept on the settee, and I haven't seen her since."

"You did the right thing, Toby," Susie said immediately. "Sometimes you just have to rip the plaster off quickly. It is sad. Gosh, you two were together for five years, but best to do it now. Drifting on for another five years won't help."

"No, your mum's correct. It had to be done. I feel sorry for Jasmine, though, she'll be beginning to realise what's she's lost just about now!" Rob smiled kindly at his son. "How do you feel at the moment, Toby?"

"I feel a bit bruised, but I think that's more because of the way that it happened, actually. Apart from that, I feel relieved. It's good to talk it through with you guys." Toby grinned at them, and looked more like his old self.

Susie gave Toby a big maternal hug. "It'll take a little while to put it behind you. The cords that you've forged between your chakras and Jasmine's have to withdraw. But that means there is a period of retrieving yourself. We're here for you, my love. If there's anything we can do, just shout."

"I know, Mum." Toby replied. "Right now, it just feels great to be home!"

Toby slept well that night and woke up with an appetite. His parents loved having him home, and spent a lot of time just chatting and laughing with him. He looked a good deal more cheerful when he left on Sunday evening.

"There, Yoga," Susie said, as she waved to Toby's car until it disappeared around the corner. "We had a lesson this weekend in how the chakras are affected when a relationship comes to an end. As for the chakra which most needs stimulating to improve our world, I'm beginning to think that it can't be just one. I think this is a trick question. The answer is that we need to balance and work with all the chakras. Just like all of humanity is interconnected, so it is with the wheels of energy."

Susie and Rob discussed this in more depth later. "You really see the range of emotions that affect the heart, and the heart chakra, when your kids are going through stuff, don't you?" Rob said.

"Oh yes," Susie agreed. "I go into the mode of 'I'd rather go through this myself than have my son upset' very readily! I have to take a step back and think, 'This is Toby's karma, this is Toby's lesson in life.' But our hearts ache to see his heart in pain!"

"Yes, that's right, but you can also almost see him rebalancing. You can tell, from the way he talked, how much he put himself aside in order to keep Jas happy. Relationships are endlessly fascinating."

"That's the truth, all right. Toby will spend the next couple of months reclaiming bits of himself, and finding a new normal. Fortunately, he's a sensible lad. He's grounded, so his root chakra is strong. He's opened up to us, so he's connected with his sacral chakra. He's inherited our willpower, and he's gained a lot of self-confidence in his job, so his solar plexus chakra is in good shape. Yes, his heart chakra is raw, because he definitely loved Jas, but that will heal. He's communicated his feelings, and he's said that he'll chat it over with Max next week, so his throat chakra's okay. As for the brow chakra, it was his intuition which led him to the right decision. He's already accepting that there's a plan for his life and that Jasmine is no longer part of that plan, so I know his crown chakra is intact. Bless him. It's hard when they're grown-up and you can no longer kiss everything better!"

Rob gave his lovely wife a big hug. "How lucky we are, sweetheart," he breathed into her hair. "I'm going to visualise Toby finding a wonderful soulmate, just like I found you. I do appreciate you, you know."

Susie smiled up at him. "I do appreciate you too, darling! Yes, we are lucky. Life is good, for all its ups and downs, and I know it will all work out for Toby."

CHAPTER 12

And Yoga asked:

"All chakras need to be balanced for humanity to thrive, but is there one which is weak at this time? In this day and age, do we need to focus on strengthening one particular wheel of energy?"

This query built on the previous one, and it came to Susie whilst she was taking a shower. She shampooed her hair whilst considering the question carefully. Susie's chestnut hair was still curly and thick. She always used a natural shampoo from the health stores – one that did not contain any SLS (sodium lauryl sulfate). She favoured an Indian soap, too, which she felt was kind to her skin. Susie recognised that taking a shower cleansed her aura as well as her physical body.

Times were changing. Politically, there was extreme unrest in the world. Global warming was a huge concern, and war, famine and disease were still prevalent. Susie felt Yoga's concern for humanity at this difficult time.

Later that day, Susie walked up to Home from OM. She found her mother, Marion, playing Scrabble with Jean, Rosie and Julia. "Are you ladies using yoga words as well?" Susie enquired.

"Oh yes," Marion laughed. "Look, we already have 'asana' and 'mat' on the board!"

"Well done!" Susie replied. "My teaching has not been completely in vain then!"

Susie was looking for either Jamila or Bernard. They were both wonderful sounding boards, and both so knowledgeable about yoga matters. She would like to run this new question past them.

She eventually tracked Bernard down. He was just coming out of the meditation hut.

"Have you time for a herbal tea, Bernard?" Susie asked.

"I certainly have," he replied readily. "My lady wife is out on a shopping trip with Pam, so I am quite at my leisure."

"What are they buying?" Susie enquired as she put on the kettle in the tea-making corner of the lounge.

"It's Pam and Jimmy's granddaughter's birthday gift that they're seeking. She's going to be eighteen, so it's a big one." Bernard sat down in one of the comfortable armchairs.

"Wow, that *is* a big one," Susie agreed, bringing the teas to the table. "Now, here's another big one. This time it's a question: 'If we were to look at humanity from a global perspective, which chakra needs strengthening to help us where we are right now?' Discuss!"

"Ah," Bernard rubbed his beard thoughtfully. "My knee-jerk reaction would be to say the heart chakra. John Lennon had it right when he said, 'All you need is love'! We're always in need of more compassion, more caring, more generosity and more gratitude, I think. But there has to be a balance. Yoga has taught me that. There are some manipulative politicians out there, and some of the citizens of the world seem determined to give us all a big shake-up. I'm not keen at all on the nationalism and protectionism that I'm witnessing on the news. I think we definitely need to keep our brow chakras in good order. We need to listen to our intuition, our inner gurus. That way, we won't be swayed by dangerous rhetoric." Bernard sipped his peppermint tea. "What are your thoughts, Susie?" he asked.

"I agree with everything you've said, Bernard. And I do feel that we need to strengthen the 'global brow chakra'. Spiritual leaders like the Dalai Lama and Archbishop Desmond Tutu are inspiring people wherever they go, but it seems to me that it's the voice of negativity that is being heard."

Bernard nodded his agreement. "Yes, and it appears that, occasionally, a leader emerges who astonishes us all. But have they, on a karmic level, volunteered to do just that? Have they come into our consciousness to make us realise how ridiculous we are all being?"

"Mm," Susie answered, "I get what you mean. Does evil have to rise to the surface, so that we can skim it off and start again?"

"When you consider the horrors that Hitler brought to the world, it chills you to the bone. I find Holocaust Memorial day so very moving. And we must never forget all those dear souls. It appals right-thinking people when you hear leaders uttering words of hate, and actually convincing the population that it's acceptable." Bernard looked grave.

"Like you, yoga has taught me balance." Susie placed her left hand on her heart. "I do recognise that in order for there to be light, there must be darkness. I do recognise that to see good, we must also be aware of evil. But, and I guess this is the dreamer in me, I've always believed that light and good would eventually dominate. I guess what I'm trying to say is that the vibrations would eventually grow higher. We may not completely eliminate evil and darkness, but somehow we would bring them closer to the light. Does that make any sense at all?"

Bernard smiled at her. "Well, to quote our friend, John Lennon again: 'You may call me a dreamer, but I'm not the only one'. I'm right there with you, Susie! There would be no reason to go on if we doubted the intrinsic goodness in most of mankind. We have to believe that goodness will prevail."

"So back we go to the initial question," Susie said. "Is it the brow chakra that needs to be strengthened, throughout all peoples? Or do we, perhaps, need to strengthen the global solar plexus? If we were all more strong-willed, would we be better equipped to resist negativity and wrong-thinking?"

"I'm sticking with the brow chakra. I have a hunch that the world has too many people with strong wills right now! I think we all need to listen, and listen hard, to the messages from our spirit guides. This time will pass." Bernard patted Susie's arm, fondly.

"You're so wise, Bernard." Susie grinned at him. "In our own little world here in Home from OM, we can live in harmony. I would not thrive in a community where discord was the norm. I will always avoid volatile and difficult people. Whilst I will totally support the idea that we are all entitled to our own opinions, and respect that, kindness in expressing those views is an essential part of being civilised."

"It's certainly not easy living with someone who is angry and looking for an argument on the thinnest of excuses," Bernard agreed, "I used to be like that, and I can tell you that it's very wearing to be that person, too!"

Just at that moment, Valerie and Pam burst into the room. "We've had so much fun!" Valerie enthused. "Shopping for an eighteen-year-old has awakened all our young dreams and wishes!"

"Mission is accomplished, too," Pam giggled. "I think we could call this a very successful event. Valerie and I had the best time, and Amelia is going to love her present! We've bought her a whole outfit – she will look fabulous!"

The next few minutes were taken up with a series of appreciative gasps as Pam displayed their purchases. Susie couldn't help hoping that Amelia would be as thrilled with her dress, jacket and shoes as Pam clearly was!

By the end of that day, Bernard's pronouncement on the brow chakra had convinced Susie. All in all, she felt that humanity needed to tune into the higher vibrations of the upper wheels of energy. She remembered the old saying that we must always remember that we are spiritual beings who are having an earthly experience. "What is abundantly clear, Yoga," she said, as she prepared for bed, "is that the world needs all the spiritual help that it can get right now!"

CHAPTER 13

And Yoga asked:

"Which of the yoga rules would you most like your sons to adhere to in their lives?"

Susie didn't need to consult with anyone on this question. "*Ahimsa*, non-violence, would be the rule that I would choose for them to follow," she replied immediately, "and I believe that Max and Toby have embraced it fully. You only have to look at how Toby has dealt with the break-up of his relationship. He hasn't said horrible things about Jasmine, and he's recognised that there were faults on both sides. Max has been a tower of strength to him, too, and he's refrained from criticising Jas, even though he was clearly protective towards his brother. In fact, Max's beautiful fiancée, Megan, has even performed the role of mediator. She has been instrumental in sorting out any disagreements over possessions."

Whilst these thoughts were playing in Susie's mind, she made her way down the corridor towards the yoga hall in Home from OM. As she opened the door, she saw Jamila carefully rescuing a spider and taking it out through the

French doors. "There, Yoga, we see non-violence in action!" Susie thought.

The practice that morning focussed on this, the first rule of yoga. It never hurt to remind the old yogis that non-violence applied to the way that they practised their asanas. "Listen to your bodies," Susie would stress. "Never push or force. Work with the three areas – that which is easy for you, as an individual, that which is challenging, and that which is painful. I never want you to hit pain."

Certainly it was easier to obey the rule of ahimsa in the home than anywhere else. The community ran on yogic values. The food was vegetarian so no creatures were killed to feed the residents. Living in a group could bring up challenges, but these were resolved lovingly. Practising yoga and meditation everyday filled everyone's minds with good thoughts, positivity, so there was no room for discord.

Maureen waited for Susie at the end of that morning's practice. "I loved that class, Susie," she began, "it's always wonderful to be reminded that gentleness with ourselves is as important as gentleness with others. I really felt dear Alice in the room today. What I realised is that Alice demonstrated positive ahimsa. With her it wasn't just that she never hurt anyone else, but she actively set out to help others. I'm feeling that I can learn from that."

"I know just what you mean, Maureen," Susie replied. "Alice embodied the first rule of yoga, non-violence, and she really seemed to have come that way! Being in the home only reinforced the behaviour that she had always demonstrated."

Maureen was a nervous lady who'd had a difficult life. She had made a special bond with Alice and still missed her.

Alice had gently supported Maureen when she had first moved into the yoga community, and Maureen keenly felt the lack of that special support since Alice had moved to Spirit World.

"Is there anything that I can get involved in, Susie? Locally, I mean. I would love to be more active in my pursuit of ahimsa. I'd like to carry forward Alice's ethos, if I can." Maureen smiled, shyly.

"I'm going to give that some thought, Maureen," Susie promised. "Let's find just the right project for you." With that, Susie gave the sweet lady a big hug and they parted.

As Susie passed through the entrance hall, she gently touched Alice's plaque. "If it hadn't been for our beautiful Alice," she thought, "there would have been no Home from OM. How incredibly generous she was to donate her own cottage and to make this venture possible."

As sometimes happens, Susie heard of a project later that day that would really suit Maureen's skills. "The universe was quick off the mark with that one," she chuckled to herself. The local school was asking for volunteers to hear the children read. This would be ideal. It would take Maureen out of herself to interact with the youngsters, and she would be so gentle and kind that even the shyest child would gain confidence.

Maureen was delighted with the suggestion. It was all set up and she began her sessions on the following Thursday. The children were reading *The Secret Garden* by Frances Hodgson Burnett. Maureen was as fascinated by the story as they were. She was so taken with it, in fact, that she popped into the local second-hand bookstore and bought a copy for herself. "I shall tell Susie about this," she thought. "This story demonstrates some of yoga's magic. And it really describes how goodness and active adherence to the first rule of yoga, ahimsa (or non-violence) can manifest changes in the world. I'm quite in love with Dickon! His character is so kind, so gentle, and so sensitive. He's an animal whisperer!"

Patanjali's *Eight Limbs* were alive and well in the yoga home. The ripples spread out into the community and into the families and friends of the old yogis. "Oh, Yoga," Susie thought, "if only the whole world would embrace Patanjali's first directive. Let's continue to believe that we can change the world, one breath at a time."

CHAPTER 14

And Yoga asked:

"Do the yogic guidelines still offer students a moral compass?"

Now and then Susie and Rob offered a quiz night in the home. All the yogis really enjoyed it, and other yoga teachers would often come too. Jane and Joanna would put on a buffet and would stay for the fun. This quiz was to be on Patanjali's *Eight Limbs*. Everyone wanted to sit next to Bernard, since he was the font of all knowledge!

"We'll start with an easy one," Susie decreed, as they all settled down with their pens and papers. "'What is the overall term for the first of the *Eight Limbs*?'"

Most of the yogis scribbled down 'yamas', but Jean got confused and put 'ahimsa'.

"Second question: 'Did Patanjali invent the *Eight Limbs*?' A one word answer is fine, but you can expand if you like."

Maureen looked puzzled. She had always thought that Patanjali had invented them, but she had caught a knowing look which had passed between Valerie and Bernard. Now she was doubting herself.

"Third question, and I don't expect anyone to get this one wrong…"

"No pressure then," laughed Rosie.

Susie continued, "'What is the Sanskrit name for non-violence?'"

Sure enough, everyone did know that answer!

"Now, fourth question: 'What is the Sanskrit name for truthfulness?' That, I imagine, is a bit tougher," Susie said, with a grin.

Bernard, Valerie and Jamila were happily scribbling their answer, 'satya', while Jimmy looked bewildered.

"Okay, this is a nice one for you: 'How do I refer to the first category in the *Eight Limbs*?' It's an expression in common speech." Susie glanced around the room. Her mother, Marion, was grinning at her. She remembered her grandsons quoting this to her when they first began children's yoga classes. "The first rules, Granny, are called the 'Don'ts'!"

"Question number six: 'What is *aparigraha*?' And question number seven: 'When might we be tempted to flout this rule?'" Susie grinned as many eyes travelled to the beautiful buffet that Jane and Joanna had prepared (*aparigraha*, of course, means non-greed!).

The quiz continued in this way with Susie referencing the 'Do's' or *niyamas*, the asanas, pranayama and the sense-withdrawal which leads us towards meditation and, eventually, bliss.

Everyone had good fun that night. Absorbing Patanjali's teachings in a light-hearted way reminded Joanna of the saying 'Enlightenment does not have to be serious!' She had an idea which she immediately wanted to share with Susie.

How about, one evening, playing that game with the post-it notes on the forehead? Each post-it could say one of the yamas or the niyamas, and the person concerned would have to guess which one they were. Susie loved the idea as soon as Joanna mentioned it. "That's great," she enthused. "Let's do that next month!"

Evenings of this sort were such a joy for all of the residents of Home from OM. The other folk who came to join them brought fresh energy and fresh ideas into their space. There was always laughter. They all went to bed in good spirits and woke the next morning filled with a sense of well-being.

Susie began to consider Yoga's question after morning practice. She felt that her parents had instilled in her a solid moral compass. When her father so suddenly left she was a bit lost, for a while, but by then she and Rob had forged a solid relationship. He saw her through that crisis. She had always felt loved by both parents, and still did even after Jim's departure. Susie had healthy self-esteem and felt grounded in her life. Yoga, of course, became her life and guided her in all her decisions. The teachings of Patanjali stood her in good stead with any of life's more difficult challenges. The *Eight Limbs* were, to her, a set of rules that were timeless.

"Would you say that you have a firm moral compass, Mum?" she asked Marion, as they took a walk around the garden.

"Yes, I would say so," Marion replied. "Your grandparents were good people and they taught me right from wrong from an early age."

"That's where I began when I started to consider this question," Susie agreed. "Even though Dad did that curious disappearing act, I always felt that the two of you guided me towards the right decisions. I really hope that Rob and I have equipped our boys with a reliable moral compass, too."

"Oh I'm sure that is the case, sweetheart," Marion said, quickly. "It's not easy for the young people to navigate their way through life nowadays, but Max and Toby are just lovely. It's what kids absorb when they're young that sees them through. I remember hearing a saying once which was something like, 'It's the things that are accepted in the home, not what children are told, that makes the strongest impression'. You've brought your twins up in a yoga household, and they learned to be true to good ethics from a very young age!"

"That's all you can hope, as a parent, isn't it? That the love you give them, and the way that you approach life, will see them through tricky times. If my moral compass is wavering, I turn to Patanjali's *Eight Limbs*. For me, they are a code for life." Susie looked earnest.

"Well, you can't go wrong once you've found your own belief system. I think I was most challenged when your dad left. We'd said our vows and I would have stood by them. Having said that, though, when I see you and Rob together I do know that we didn't share that sort of love. And now, when I hear Valerie and Bernard chuckling together, and holding hands under the table, I do recognise that Jim and I were ill-suited. I didn't lose my way, when he left, I was just a bit bewildered." Marion looked at her daughter and smiled.

"I'm sorry that you didn't have a more loving marriage, Mum," Susie replied, a little sadly.

"Well, gosh," Marion said, "I'm the luckiest person I know! I may not have had the love of my life, but Jim and I made you! I've had the best daughter in the world; the best son-in-law in the world; and the best two grandsons in the world! I count myself to be very fortunate. My life has not been without love."

"Bless you," Susie answered. "So, do you think that your start in life is what determines how solid your moral compass is? I feel so strongly that children should all have access to yoga classes in school. If we were all brought up with the *Eight Limbs*, regardless of religion or culture, society would have a working model. I believe that right and wrong would be clarified completely."

"Yet we need to be tolerant of other people's views, Susie," Marion looked thoughtful. "There's always a range. Even within Patanjali's *Eight Limbs* there is room for personal interpretation. For instance, let's look at *aparigraha*: non-greed. To one person that might mean not eating two cream cakes, to another person it could become their life's work. They could become obsessed with not using up the earth's resources. They could lead an entirely green life – not driving a vehicle, never flying away on holiday. They could become strict vegans, determined never to harm another creature. They could take the rule of non-greed into every aspect of their lives. So there we see one rule, but different reactions."

"Yes, you're right, Mum. The teachings of yoga, for me, offer all the answers, but I still run them past my common sense. I want to change the world, one breath at a time, but I must recognise that there are folk who don't agree with me. Right now, politically, there seems to be a number of world leaders who don't have a recognisable moral compass. It's been good to see such a healthy reaction with protest marches, and comments on social media. People are running statements past their own moral compasses and finding others who feel similarly about what is right and what is wrong."

"To me it seems that we must all light a candle in our own corner of the world. Right and wrong can always be interpreted differently. There's the example of someone stealing a loaf of bread. That would be wrong. But suppose that person is stealing a loaf of bread because otherwise his children would starve. Then the stealing of the loaf is still wrong, but now it's better than letting children starve. Surely we have to bring in compassion, understanding and dialogue wherever there is a moral dilemma?" Marion sat down on the garden bench and gazed at the magnolia tree, which was displaying its large pink flowers.

"Dialogue is crucial, isn't it?" Susie agreed. "I heard recently that Holland always has a coalition government. That way, everything has to be discussed and agreed. That's so clever. Going back to our starting point, it's healthy discussion in the home, and what the children see around them, which provides them with a firm moral compass. Thanks, Mum, for mine!"

"Well," Marion laughed, "I think I had good material to work with! I read once that you cannot teach honour and integrity. It's either there or it's not."

"I suppose that's in the genes, too! We *could* get into karma, reincarnation and religion, but I just heard the gong for your lunch! Come on, I'll walk you in."

Susie and Marion parted with a special hug at the dining room door.

"Thank you for that question, Yoga," Susie thought. "Considering you have been around for five thousand years, you are remarkably up-to-date!"

CHAPTER 15

And Yoga asked:

"What about your own personal growth? What are you working on, spiritually, at the moment?"

Susie was taking Kitty Kara to the vet. Her annual check-up and inoculations were due. Kara was not at all impressed. She deeply resented being thrust into the wicker basket, and she came out with feline swear words that Susie hadn't heard before! The car journey to the surgery was not a peaceful one, but on arrival Kara was so daunted by the smells and sounds of the reception that she became quite speechless. The vet was lovely – kind but firm – and Kara was pronounced to be in perfect health. The little cat was quiet on the way home, somehow sensing that the drama was near its completion. Never was a cat more pleased to be released from her basket! Susie opened it in the lounge, and Kara strutted off, demonstrating her indignation with every step. She found a corner of the room where the sun was pouring in, sat down and gave herself a thorough wash.

Rosie walked in at that moment. "Oh good," Susie said, "here comes your favourite lap, Kara. She's affronted, Rosie. I've just taken her to the vet for her check-up."

"Bless her," Rosie sat down immediately. "Come on, come to Rosie. We'll have a cuddle and settle you down."

Kara sprang nimbly on to Rosie's comfortable lap and entered into a long conversation about her experience. Susie left them there with a smile. Pet energy around Home from OM was an integral part of its healing atmosphere.

Walking back home, Susie gave some thought to Yoga's current query. "Letting go is still a big issue for me, Yoga. It pops up in my life on a regular basis. I found it very hard to let go of dear Alice, and now I'm working to let go of Toby. Where your children are concerned, it's a mother's instinct to fix everything for them. Of course, when they're tiny, their hurts are brief. They fall over and you pick them up, give them a cuddle and rub them better. When they're grown, their difficulties are so much more complicated. Toby needed us when his relationship foundered. Now, he's doing pretty well and I must let him go. I find that quite difficult. When they need you it's all really urgent. You must drop everything and be there. Then, when they no longer need you, off they go and you're left feeling a bit shell-shocked."

Susie went into Wellness Within to check on the yoga studio and therapy rooms. She had a brief moment when she thought what fun it would have been to have had a daughter; someone who would have continued the work here. One thing was for certain – neither of the boys were going to take their yoga teacher training. "I guess that's another example of letting go, Yoga," Susie mused. "I need to face the fact that, one day, I will have to pass all this on." A moment of sadness swept over her, but she laughed out loud at herself. "Oh goodness, I just need to trust that you and the universe will sort it all out for me!"

There was no more time for introspection as some of Susie's students began to arrive for their weekly class. She was soon involved in hugs and chatter.

During the long relaxation, Susie returned to the issue of letting go. She recognised that relaxation was teaching them all to do just that. Every yoga class completed with a big release, which Susie sometimes described as a holiday for the nervous system. She had learnt that she must let go of her students, too. Some, of whom she had become really fond, moved away or became unwell. Her classes all contained a strong group of regulars, but there were new students arriving and changing the energies, which was actually beneficial for all.

A fairly new student, Margaret, waited to talk to Susie at the end. She was very concerned about her mother who had recently been moved into a care home. Margaret was struggling with guilt. Had she made the right decision? Was this the right place for her mother? Susie listened to all her concerns in a supportive and sympathetic way, whilst realising that here too was an issue of letting go. "I just feel awful every time I leave her," Margaret said. "I want to tuck her under my arm and take her home with me." Her eyes filled with tears.

"Are the people in the home kind to your mother, Margaret?" Susie enquired.

"Oh yes, they're wonderful with her really. And she has good medical support, so I know in my heart of hearts that she's where she should be." Margaret still looked beset with fears. "I suppose I just feel that I've let her down in some way. I should have her at home. I should be nursing her."

"Turn your mind back several years, Margaret," Susie advised. "What would your mum say in answer to your concerns?"

Margaret looked thoughtful. "She would say, 'You've always done your best for me, Margaret. I'm at the end of my life and I've had a good one. We'll see this through together, so don't fret. What will be, will be.' She always said that. Of course, now her speech is confused and she speaks so quietly that it's hard to make out her words." A tear escaped from Margaret's eye.

"Your mum sounds like a very practical lady," Susie said reassuringly. "You must really miss your chats with her. It's so difficult for you, she's still here but yet she's gone, too."

"That's right," Margaret agreed. "Bless her, it breaks my heart to see her going downhill so rapidly."

"And this too shall pass, Margaret," Susie gave her a big hug. "There's a lovely American saying for you to ponder: 'Worry is like a rocking-chair. It goes back and forth but gets you nowhere.' Your mum wouldn't want you to be consumed with worry."

"You're right, Susie," Margaret replied. "Thank you, I feel a bit better after talking to you."

Susie walked Margaret to the door. Pastoral care is a large part of a yoga teacher's role, and Susie had good people skills. As she went next door for her lunch, Susie pondered on how professional and detached a yoga teacher must be in order to provide the appropriate amount of support. "I've become quite good at that aspect of letting go over the years, Yoga. My tutor drummed it into me that if I took on everyone's problems wholesale, I would soon become drained. Then I wouldn't have the energy to teach and to support. It's all the same lesson, isn't it? I guess really that it's about trusting. Adhere to your moral compass, make the best decisions you can, trust in the right outcome and don't be afraid to let go."

CHAPTER 16

And Yoga said:

"Does your spiritual growth have an impact on the progress of your students? Indeed, how does your method of operation affect them?"

"Now that's a good one, Yoga!" Susie thought, with approval. This question had arrived during the long relaxation at the end of the early morning practice. This was a time when Susie was 'wide open'. "In the case of the old yogis here in Home from OM, my spiritual growth has quite a deep effect. We live along together and I'm responsible for their well-being. If I reach a realisation that would be useful for them, I implement it immediately. I suppose that is also true of my weekly students, although they have lives away from yoga and the yoga community, so my messages are likely to be diluted by every-day cares. Your question makes me feel very responsible! It's a daunting prospect, Yoga!"

Susie invited her group to dissolve their relaxation practice and to roll onto their sides. "When you're ready, open your eyes and come back to this room and back to the world," Susie said, softly.

Marion caught Susie's eye across the room and smiled, lazily.

After rolling up their mats, the residents of the old yogis' home made their way to breakfast. Susie went into the kitchen to talk to Joanna. "Am I bossy?" Susie asked her, without any preamble.

Joanna smiled at her, surprised by the abrupt question. "No, I wouldn't have said you were bossy, Susie. You're certainly firm in your views. You have a strong sense of what is right and what is wrong. Why do you ask?"

"Do I have a problem taking advice?" Susie ignored Joanna's question and ploughed on.

"No, I wouldn't say that you have a problem with accepting advice or suggestions, although you would always run them past your own common sense. You're certainly not a doormat!"

"I suppose the danger of being the yoga teacher and the owner of Home from OM is that I become some sort of benevolent dictator! I would hate the oldies to think that I was even the tiniest bit bullying!" Susie looked closely at Joanna to see if she understood.

Joanna laughed. "You have nothing to worry about, dear Susie!" Joanna came around the kitchen island and gave her a hug. "I don't know where this has come from, but I would have described you as the most positive and loving person that I have ever met. You're an inspiration, not a bully! You live by the yogic ethics and you run this home from a place of goodness. Why are you experiencing misgivings this fine morning?"

"Well," Susie admitted, "it was a query from Headquarters! In my heart I know that it was a little nudge to remind me that my spiritual progress is important to all of us here. And, of course, it was to remind me to make time for my own practice. I do try to do that, and I always have a meditation first thing in the morning, but sometimes life is pretty hectic and time is short. It's essential for me to believe that I'm coming from the right place, from the heart."

"There is no doubt about that, Susie," Joanna replied. "We've been friends for a long time now. I would certainly tell you if I thought you were off-beam. It's an important point, though. Your energy influences all of us here. Your spiritual progress matters. Do you think you might occasionally need to go on retreat? Elly attends one every year, and she swears by it. She feels that her yoga students really benefit, as she comes back refreshed and renewed."

"That's a good thought, Joanna," Susie looked pensive. "I think I just had a strong realisation about the responsibility of being the yoga teacher. It's humbling. It's daunting. It's a huge privilege, of course, and I love all my charges, but I'm still just an imperfect human being!"

"It sounds to me like you need a good laugh!" Joanna replied. "You're taking yourself too seriously. There's nothing wrong with you, Susie, other than a healthy dose of self-doubt!"

Susie had to grin. She thanked the universe for a friend like Joanna.

In all, Susie taught thirteen practices per week. Ten of these were at the home and three were at her yoga centre, Wellness Within. She had been considering setting up a meditation group there too. She determined to go ahead with that plan. It would be good for her, and it would be good for others. That week, she watched herself carefully. Joanna could be right. It may be that she needed to schedule in a retreat.

"Sometimes, Yoga, you give me a well needed shove," she thought. "You provide the grain of sand in the shell, which irritates, but finally produces a pearl. Thank you for reminding me that my spiritual progress is important for everyone. This, of course, is true for each person in the community, not just me. We're in this together. We all have an effect on one another – physically, mentally, emotionally and spiritually. That's the whole point of living in a community."

- PART TWO -

SUSIE TURNS IT AROUND

CHAPTER 17

And Susie asked:

"Yoga, what do you think about protection? I know that some yoga teachers think it's very important to close down the chakras after a practice. What are your thoughts?"

Susie asked this question of Yoga – her mentor, guide and best-friend, during the long relaxation at the end of the early morning practice. She found this to be a time when she was most open and responsive so their dialogue flowed freely.

"I believe that our chakras should be open and spinning freely all the time," Yoga replied. "Our yoga practice takes us to a meditative place where we can access Spirit World. We then take down the high vibrations, action them through our wheels of energy, and send them out into the world."

"Is there ever a time when we should protect ourselves?" Susie continued.

"Yes, there are times when protection is necessary. If someone was compelled to spend time with others who are manifesting a negative, destructive energy, it would be appropriate to protect the aura. There are many ways to do this. The easiest and quickest way is to say, 'nine times nine' in the mind. That provides you with instant protection. Some people like to imagine themselves surrounded by a strong force field; this can allow positive energy to move outwards, but prevents negative energy entering."

"I turn to 'nine times nine' and it really seems to work for me, but I've heard of people who imagine building a wall in front of them, and others who imagine that they are surrounded by an egg of loving energy. Should you then, if you felt that you were being drained or spiritually attacked, close down your chakras, Yoga?" Susie asked.

"I still believe that the chakras need to be open. If you are dealing with an 'energy pirate' who is attempting to drain you, they always target the solar plexus chakra. You can block this by folding your arms in front of that wheel."

"What about if you were to leave a beautiful, spiritual practice and then go out into a bustling, hectic city centre. Wouldn't you be too open?" Susie persisted.

"All good yoga teachers bring their students around from the relaxation, and give them time to come back into the world. A natural rebalancing will occur. But think about the great energy that the yogi is taking out into the city! What a gift that would be. I would say that thoughts of giving rather than receiving would be the key here. If we're focussed on giving our energies for the good of all, we're not concerned about being attacked. This may tie in with the anxiety and stress which is rife in the world. People may fear that their chakras are too open."

"I see what you mean, Yoga," Susie replied, in her mind. "I have always felt that, on a deep level, the greeting 'Namaste' opens us up to the work, and the farewell 'OM Shanti Shanti Shanti' brings closure."

"That's true, and yogis trust that they're being watched over by their guardian angels and spirit guides. But, having said all that, there may not be a right way or a wrong way. Rather it is important to listen to yourself. Yoga is, after all, a journey of self-discovery. If ever an occasion arose where a yogi felt the need to gently close down the lotus flowers of their chakras they could do so. There would be no harm done, and they could soon reopen them."

"Thank you for your insights, Yoga," Susie mentally replied.

It was Marion who waited for Susie after the class that morning. "How's Toby doing, Susie?" she asked.

"Very well, thanks Mum," she replied. "Max and Megan have been really supportive, and he's putting it all behind him. It's hard to cope with a break-up, but I know I can't wrap him in cotton wool. He has to learn his lessons."

"I'm glad he's doing all right," Marion said. "His soulmate is out there somewhere. He's only young and there's plenty of time."

"That's very true," Susie agreed. "I'm finding it hard to believe that one of our boys is going to be married! Where does the time go?"

"Have we any idea of a date yet? Am I looking for a summer outfit or a winter one?" Marion asked.

"I've no idea yet, Mum, but you'll be the first person I tell when I do know!"

Susie went home, collected the post from the door mat, and put on the kettle. It interested her that Toby had recovered so well from his broken relationship. She took it as a sign that he and Jasmine had worked out their karma with one another, and both recognised that it was time to move on. Susie could see that we all have to be open in order for a relationship to be possible. Here was an area where people have to be brave and just go for it. Yoga was correct, it was a matter of trust. Toby's chakras were rebalancing and, in time, he would love again.

CHAPTER 18

And Susie asked:

*"What about the gaps between the chakras, Yoga?
Is there work to be done there?"*

Susie had again chosen the time at the end of her first class to ask this question. She was feeling particularly light that morning, having woken early and experienced a wonderful phenomenon. She returned to it now. It had taken place in the first moments of waking, before Susie got up to meditate, so her eyes were still closed. She'd heard a beautiful song. It was haunting but not sad. The voice was female, confident and joyful. Both the music and the words were unfamiliar to Susie, but they touched her deeply. The knowledge came into her consciousness that it was her heart singing! She kept this occurrence close to her, not wanting to share it with anyone just yet, but the sense of 'all is well' that came with it lingered on.

"This is definitely the case, Susie," Yoga replied. "There is work to be done between the chakras because this is the area of transition. Moving from the root chakra to the sacral chakra, learning takes place. We move from a focus of survival to an enjoyment of being physical. Although we talk about the seven main chakras, there are other smaller ones too, of course."

"Yes, that's right. Although we teach mainly about the seven main chakras, we mustn't forget the smaller ones. While each main chakra is located at a major nerve plexus of the body and is intricately involved in keeping the organs in that area in perfect balance, the smaller ones must be performing a similar service, perhaps in a more subtle way."

"The energy field is a most fascinating subject. I hear that many people describe the aura now as the eighth chakra," Yoga replied.

Susie was to return to her thoughts of the chakras many times that day, and each time that she did, Yoga fed her a fresh insight.

"Each chakra is fed by prana, Susie. Keeping the energy wheels belonging to your old yogis spinning freely is essential. If a chakra is not functioning correctly, eventually that part of the body will begin to close down. It will become uneasy, and begin to harbour disease."

Susie regularly checked her own chakras. Her preferred method of bringing her energy wheels into perfect balance was by chanting the seed sounds. These sounds relate to each of the seven main chakras. Susie would begin at the root chakra, move up to the crown chakra, and then do the reverse. This she could do silently, or out-loud. Rob was quite accustomed to hearing 'Lam, Vam, Ram, Yam, Ham, OM, Soham' coming from the bathroom, while Susie took a shower!

"Could it be that other sounds bring the smaller chakras into balance, Yoga?" she queried. "Perhaps the Gayatri Mantra does just this."

"This is definitely the case," Yoga confirmed. "Chanting is more profound than most people realise. It stems from *bhakti yoga* (the yoga of devotion), but it's enormously helpful for *raja yoga* (the yoga of meditation), and it leads us to *karma yoga* (the yoga of selfless service). This world is determined to investigate everything. There is a heavy emphasis on all things scientific. Yoga stands up to such scrutiny, but still keeps some magic in its practices. It's surely important to combine such activities as chanting with a healthy dose of trust. If students feel lighter and more energetic after chanting, then they can trust that the chants have activated their major and minor chakras."

Susie walked into the dining room at lunchtime and surveyed the scene. The residents of Home from OM were all chatting vivaciously. Clearly their chakras were firing on all cylinders! Susie stood for a moment and watched her mother. Marion was conversing with Valerie. They had been friends for a long time and very much enjoyed one another's company. Susie felt a rush of joy to observe how happy her mother was in this elderly community.

Joanna called Susie at that moment from the kitchen. "Did you know that it was Miles's birthday tomorrow, Susie?" Joanna asked.

"Oh my word, that's crept up on me quickly!" Susie replied. "Any thoughts on how we'll celebrate the special day, Joanna?"

"Well, I was talking it over with Jane. We're thinking of doing an Italian evening. After all, Miles and his partner ran an Italian restaurant for many, many years, so it would bring back happy memories."

"That's brilliant," Susie agreed. "Write me a shopping list and I'll nip out this afternoon and get the supplies. I shall have to come up with a clever gift, too."

In the event, Susie found an excellent book on the chakras for Miles. She sneaked around and managed to get everyone to sign the inside of the book. Miles was delighted when he opened it. He loved the Italian meal of vegetarian lasagne with garlic bread, followed by zabaglione for dessert. They covered the tables with red and white checked cloths and played Italian music. Miles had a splendid time. Rising to his feet after the dessert, he thanked everyone warmly.

"It's such a privilege to live amongst you all," he declared. "Thank you so much for making my birthday so special. I feel really spoilt!"

All the heart chakras were open that evening as the old yogis celebrated their friend!

Late that evening, Susie asked Yoga more about the gaps between the chakras. "The energy that feeds into the chakra points of the main wheels of energy looks like a vortex," Yoga explained. "This funnel-like swirl of energy is present in the front of the body, and then there is another funnel in the back. Now, when the energy wheels are spinning freely, the glands situated at these points are fully stimulated. So, for instance, the energy entering the solar plexus chakra stimulates the adrenal glands. The energy circulating around the adrenals will leak out into the neighbouring tissues. The whole area comes alive."

"I completely get this, Yoga," Susie commented. "When I give my students a practice on the chakras, I literally see them revitalise. I can see the deep effect on their entire beings. The energy seems to swirl through them and recharge them physically, mentally, emotionally and spiritually. It's like alchemy! In comes the prana, and the yogis convert it to workable fuel for all areas."

"That's a good description, Susie," Yoga agreed.

Susie talked about the spaces between the chakras in her next few practices. It was a new approach for her elderly residents and they very much enjoyed it. The space between the heart chakra and the throat chakra became a topic of conversation during meals.

Jean asked Maureen, "Have you ever felt that expressing the emotions in your heart somehow got stuck in your throat?"

"Oh, I've felt that so often. I've always been shy, anyway, and speaking out is a real challenge for me." Maureen smiled at Jean. "You're confident though, Jean. Has that been a problem for you, too?"

"Yes it has," Jean replied. "I think, to an extent, it's the human condition. All our fears and anxieties show up when we endeavour to express ourselves emotionally. I suppose that it's fear of rejection, fear of being needy, and fear of burdening others. I remember Susie once saying that the neck is literally a bottle-neck. It filters thoughts from the mind travelling down to the body, and it filters feedback from the body to the mind. There's a lot of congestion in that small space!"

Miles was sitting with Jean and Maureen, and he now joined in the conversation. "I believe you ladies are still rather better at this than us men," he admitted. "I didn't 'do' emotions at all until I met Marco. I believe that a mixture of being a guy and being British contributed to my reticence."

"That's true," Jean agreed. "My husband was the most unromantic man on the planet! I knew that he loved me, but that love was shown by actions, rather than words."

"So do you think that, as a nation, we might have more throat problems, or upper chest problems, because of our reserve?" Maureen pondered. "It would be really interesting to compare statistics with other countries, and between the sexes, too. After all, Susie explains that blocked energy results in physical illness and disease."

"Well," suggested Miles, "we could do some interesting market research right here in the home. Granted, there's only three men, but it would still be an interesting study."

The ladies nodded in agreement. Susie, who was walking through the dining room at this moment, enjoyed seeing all the residents in earnest conversation.

"Thank you, Yoga," she said in her head. "Your answer to my question has opened up a new avenue of practice and discussion for my students. Yoga is eternally fresh."

CHAPTER 19

And Susie asked:

"How important is it for my elderly yogis to cleanse their auras? I'm wondering if living in a yoga community is actually self-cleansing in some way?"

Rosie still received the privilege of Kitty Kara's company. Her lap was the chosen one for the little cat, even when others were available. Everyone in the home had become completely used to seeing the two together, and so it was that Rosie's first symptoms of illness passed them all by. Susie did eventually become aware that Rosie was losing weight. When she asked Rosie about it her explanation seemed valid. "I've noticed it too, Susie, and I'm delighted! I've always been on the plump side, but now my clothes are spacious. I'm putting it down to long-term yoga practice and the volunteer work that I'm doing at the theatre. We're rushing up and down those steps constantly!"

Susie could tell that Rosie was enjoying being freer in her postures. Her nose-to-knee pose was now excellent. Had

Kara been sitting on anyone else's knee, it would have alerted Susie to impending illness. As it was, no-one was alarmed.

However, Rosie's weight continued to reduce, and then other symptoms manifested themselves. She began to lack energy. Certain food stuffs made her feel uncomfortable. When Rosie experienced pain in the abdomen, she determined to see Dr Iyer.

"It's probably nothing, Dr Iyer, but I thought it was wise to check with you," Rosie said.

The doctor checked her out and was concerned by her set of symptoms.

"I'm going to refer you to a specialist for some tests, Rosie," he said. "It's important to get a diagnosis, but meanwhile just keep doing what you're doing. I know Susie will keep a good eye on you."

When Rosie's appointment came through, Susie went with her to the hospital. She had time to think while Rosie was having her tests. Susie was determined to stay upbeat for Rosie, but she was beginning to suspect that the diagnosis might be bleak.

This proved to be the case. Rosie had terminal pancreatic cancer. There was nothing that the medical staff could offer, except pain relief. Rosie was remarkably calm when she received the news. As she said to Susie, when they shared a hug, "I've lived a good life. I never married or had children, but I took good care of my parents. I'm in my eighties and I've enjoyed long friendships, travel, being a teacher, and these wonderful years here in Home from OM, Susie. I have no complaints, so don't cry for me."

Rosie and Kitty Kara settled down to seeing the illness through to the end. The other residents were loving and supportive, and Rosie was the recipient of many a tender hug. On one occasion, when she was particularly poorly and stayed in bed, her fellow yogis sat cross-legged outside her room and chanted the Gayatri Mantra.

"Rosie is much beloved," Susie said to Marion as they shared a tea-break in the communal sitting room. "She's being so brave, bless her heart. I do hope that the end is kind and that she passes peacefully to Spirit World."

Marion nodded her agreement. "I can't imagine the home without her, to tell you the truth, but the years go by. It will come to us all."

"Yes, you're right, Mum," Susie agreed. "I do know that what makes the transition as smooth as possible is that we are loved at the moment of passing. As a single lady, Rosie would not have had family members to 'love her across'. I'm delighted that she has spent the last part of her life here with us. We're all her family now."

Rosie stayed unbelievably placid throughout her ordeal. She was an inspiration to them all. She had faded to a shadow of herself, and felt like a mere skeleton when hugged. The last time she came down to the lounge, Joanna and Susie got out photographs of her time with them. She smiled at the ones of her with her dear friend, Phyllis. She held on to the one of her doing the tree posture with Jamila. They were both laughing. She brought the one of the whole group, taken just after Bernard and Valerie got married, to her heart. When she was too tired for any more talking, she looked around all of them and said, "Thank you all so much for being my friends. I love you dearly."

There were few dry eyes that evening. Rosie had always been a lively member of their group and she would be sorely missed.

It was three months to the day from the diagnosis to her death. Rob held Susie tightly as, once again, she mourned one of her old yogis.

"You know, darling, it was quite beautiful really," Rob murmured. "Rosie had time to say her goodbyes. She had time to put her affairs in order. She was a neat lady, and that was important to her."

"I know," Susie agreed. "We're all going to miss her so much, though, and Kara's going to be completely lost."

Rosie's funeral was really special. Jamila read a piece by Kahlil Gibran, and Bernard read a poem to which they had all contributed. It was a sombre little group that returned to the home that day. Maureen looked devastated. She fiddled with her black gloves in her lap, and her eyes kept filling with tears.

Julia put her arms around Maureen and held her close. She could feel her shoulders shaking with silent sobs. "Remember what Susie said, Maureen," she whispered. "Love her across to the other side. Then hold her in your heart always."

"I will," Maureen sobbed, "and I keep thinking that Alice will be there to welcome her."

"Yes, she certainly will be. And, do you know what? Her parents would also have been there, waiting for her. She won't be alone." Julia squeezed Maureen a little harder, but then released her gently.

Kitty Kara seemed to instinctively understand what had occurred. She had been Rosie's constant companion throughout her three-month illness, but she no longer cried at Rosie's door. Instead, she sought Maureen out in the lounge. They found a way of comforting one another.

Susie taught classes on letting go, as she had done when Alice died. She glanced around her subdued students and wondered afresh about their auras. During one meditation, she looked at each yogi and checked the colours around them. Each aura was a little closer to their bodies than normal. Each aura was duller than usual. Their auras were demonstrating their mourning.

During the long relaxation at the end of this practice, Susie repeated her question to Yoga: "Do the old yogis need to cleanse their auras?"

"Everyone needs to cleanse their auras," Yoga replied. "Taking a shower is an efficient way to accomplish this. Living in a nourishing community, such as this one, ensures that the auras are healthy. Practising yoga and meditation each day means that the energy vibrations are kept high. Certainly the elderly yogis are feeding one another with good energy, and because the energies are pooled, all the auras receive the benefit. I enjoy your question, Susie. I would say that, yes, being surrounded by other yogis does indeed ensure that all the auras are bright and clear."

"And when Rosie arrived in Spirit World," Susie pondered, "did the work she had done on keeping her aura clean stand her in good stead?"

"Yes, Rosie's spiritual progress was fully appreciated. You don't need to worry. Rosie is exactly where she needs to be right now and she's being well looked after."

"Thank you, Yoga," Susie looked relieved. "Sometimes I just need to check that I'm doing my best for all my lovely elderly yogis."

CHAPTER 20

And Susie asked:

> *"Is there any specific age group which most benefits from yoga practice?"*

During her career, Susie had taught children's yoga classes, teenage yoga classes and adult yoga classes; now, her particular emphasis was on the elderly. She had observed how the practice had supported all age groups in different ways. Now she was interested to hear Yoga's opinion on the subject.

"I am very pleased to observe how children are embracing the practice and the philosophy," Yoga replied. "It is essential to give children a solid foundation, and a working knowledge of yoga's beliefs. They live in such a fast world – yoga will give them the means to access the peace of their inner selves. The best gift a child can receive is to live in a yoga family. There they can grow up watching the yoga way of life in practice."

"I so agree with you," Susie said, "and I've noticed that the children I taught have grown up with a desire to serve. They have absorbed the lesson of karma yoga. The *Eight*

Limbs have taught them about kindness and truthfulness. Even if life separates them from their yoga for a while, they come back to it later."

"Making yoga available to the next generation is essential. They have a difficult time to face right now. We can support them. However, all age groups need the practice. The reasons change, but yoga is perennial. It offers all age groups tools and techniques for living." Susie knew that Yoga was right about this.

Max was coming home that weekend. Susie had brought up her two sons to understand the yogic teachings. They had turned out to be responsible, hard-working young men. They were honourable and demonstrated integrity in their interactions with others. Now that Max was about to get married, Rob and Susie were seeing the strength of his character even more clearly. They were very much looking forward to seeing him.

"What time is Max arriving?" Rob asked.

"He said about eight o'clock on Friday evening," Susie replied.

"It'll be lovely to see him. I love Megan dearly, but it will be rather nice to catch up with him on his own," Rob admitted.

"I was thinking just the same thing," Susie agreed. "Isn't it lovely that they came up with this idea. Megan is spending quality time with her folks, and Max is coming home to us. They are a truly caring couple."

Sure enough, Max arrived shortly after eight o'clock. He looked well and happy, and was clearly delighted to see his parents. They spent the evening catching up, laughing and just enjoying being together. Susie was glad that she had decided not to invite her mother, Marion, tempting as it had been. Max would spend time with Marion the next day when they were all going out to lunch.

"How are the preparations going for the wedding then, Max?" Susie asked him.

"Actually, it's all going rather well," he replied. "Megan has chosen her dress. She's very excited about it, but, of course, I am to know nothing! Toby and I have started to think about our outfits. Oh – and Megan will sort out the bridesmaids dresses with her mum this weekend."

"Ooh, how lovely," Susie beamed. "How many bridesmaids are you having?"

"We're having three. Megan's best friend will be supervising her two little nieces. They're aged six and four and they're really cute kids. No doubt there will be much talk this weekend about baskets of flowers, headdresses and so on. Megan has a good eye for detail. I'm bemused by the number of decisions that need to be made!" Max grinned.

"I know what you mean, son," Rob said. "There's a sort of marriage machine that takes over the moment that you get down on one knee! But the ladies thrive on it."

"Have you thought about your outfit yet, Mum?" Max enquired.

"Not really, although I do feel that I should be talking to Megan's mum. As the mother of the bride, I need to consult her on colours. The last wedding we went to was Bernard and Valerie's. I must tell you some sad news though, my love. Dear Rosie died." Susie watched Max's face change.

"I'm really sorry to hear that," he said immediately. "It always felt to me that Rosie was ageless, and somehow permanent. I bet everyone is really missing her. How's Granny taking it?"

"She's very philosophical about it. I would describe her mood as 'resigned'. But there's definitely a Rosie-shaped hole in the yoga community. She was such a character. We all loved her dearly. She was looking forward to your wedding, and I'm absolutely sure that she will be looking down from Spirit World on that day!" Susie smiled at her son.

"Will you do something in the garden for Rosie as a remembrance, Mum?" Max enquired.

"Yes, we're trying to get our heads round that at the moment. She just loved the meditation hut, and she and Jamila had plans for the garden surrounding it." Susie looked thoughtful.

"Well, if you need any muscle power, just shout. I'd really like to do that for Rosie," Max said.

"I shall bear that in mind. Bless you. Now, tell me, how's your brother doing? We've been impressed when we've spoken to him on the phone. He does seem to be really chipper now. You'll know better than us, though, how he really is," Susie said.

Max was able to reassure his parents that Toby was doing really well. He was getting out and about with his friends and had taken a lodger to help with the bills.

Susie thought some more about her question to Yoga as she settled down to sleep. "I wonder if Max and Megan would bring up their children in the yoga way?" she mused. "That would make four generations of yogis in our family. It would be an interesting study."

Yoga was ready with more comments the following morning. Susie had completed her own meditation practice, and was thinking about making breakfast. "Max's age group need their yoga practice. The world is demanding for young people, and they don't always make time to return to their inner selves."

"This is true, Yoga, but, as you said before, the best start in life is to live in a yoga family. Max grew up with two parents who practice and live the yoga life." Susie moved around the kitchen preparing breakfast as she considered.

"Hi Mum," Max said as he appeared ready for the day. "Are we going to lunch at Home from OM? I've got a small gift for Granny from Megan and me."

"Yes, we are. Joanna said all will be ready for one o'clock and I know Granny will be looking forward to seeing you. Scrambled eggs okay?"

The morning flashed by with much chat and laughter. Rob and Max teased Susie until finally she threatened to wear a bin bag to the wedding, if they didn't stop! They walked up to the home in very good spirits and Marion was waiting for them in the hall.

Engulfing his little grandmother in a huge hug, Max declared, "Gosh, you look younger than ever! This yoga lark is really suiting you, Granny!"

Marion laughed. "Oh yes, I love living here, Max. Your mother does a wonderful job of looking after us all."

All the other residents were hovering, ready to greet their visitor, and it was a merry lunchtime for all. The weather was sunny so they all sat in the garden. Max repeated his offer to his mother. "I'll be delighted to help with the digging for Rosie's memorial, Mum."

Jamila pricked up her ears. "Ah, that's just what we need – some muscle power," she laughed. "I have some ideas, Max. Rosie and I talked about creating a chakra garden, but of course the challenge is having the colours in different plants throughout the year. Spring is straightforward. We'll plant bulbs in the autumn and they'll give us a lovely colourful display. I love the idea of having a growing and changing memorial to our dear friend. She was so open to growth." Jamila's face clouded.

Just at that moment, Kitty Kara appeared. It was almost as though she knew they were talking about her special person. The little cat walked purposely towards the meditation hut and began to scratch at the earth to the right of it.

"Well," grinned Max, "it looks as though we have another volunteer for the digging!"

Rob and Susie waved their son off later that day, then collapsed into chairs to watch the news. "What a great weekend," Rob said. "It was so good to see Max and to catch up. I'm very proud of him."

"Yes," Susie smiled, "I can't help feeling that Megan has made a really excellent choice. She, like me, has good taste in husbands!"

It was bedtime when Yoga made his final comment on Susie's question. "Yoga is for everyone. Each age group needs a structure and belief system to live by. The magic of yoga practice reaches out, like fingers, to all people. The benefits help not only those who practise, but every person and creature around them."

"Thank you, Yoga," Susie thought, as she drifted into a deep sleep.

CHAPTER 21

And Susie asked Yoga:

"Tell me about the inspirational figures that we have in the world. I'm interested in people like the Dalai Lama and Archbishop Desmond Tutu. They seem to me to be 'Joy Ambassadors'. Do you send them down that way, or is it their practice of meditation and prayer that makes them joyful?"

Susie issued her query on first waking. She felt particularly joyful that morning. The early sun was streaming through the window and her day stretched out in front of her. Susie felt at peace with the world. The challenge was to stay in that place of joy, despite the petty irritations which were bound to occur.

Yoga spoke to her during her personal meditation time. "Some evolved souls have made a great deal of progress in former lives. They are already predisposed to be positive and loving. It takes courage to come back to Planet Earth. They have a mission to help mankind, so they return bringing the light with them, and share that light with others. Certainly their daily practice of prayer and meditation takes them to a place of joy, but intention is involved, too."

"I see what you mean," Susie replied. "Often a student will ask me about this. They experience joy at the end of their yoga class, but how do they hold on to that in the busy world?"

"Once the intention is set, it becomes easier. Then it is practice, practice and more practice. In theory, once someone has seen the light, there is no returning to darkness."

Susie moved quietly through her day bearing this conversation in mind. She observed her old yogis. They were an inspiring group. Jimmy had moments of low mood, but the others soon had him laughing again. Susie was aware that she must soon open Home from OM to a new resident. Rosie had passed to Spirit World two months before, and her room was vacant and waiting.

"Hi Joanna," Susie greeted her long-time friend in the lively kitchen of the home. "Why am I reluctant to fill Rosie's room?"

"Oh, I think that's perfectly natural, Susie," Joanna replied. "You needed time to grieve, as did everyone else. Rosie was a great character, and she was one of the first residents. Has anyone tried to tell Phyllis, by the way?" Phyllis had been a much-loved resident, until the onset of dementia had made it necessary for her to move to a specialised care home. They missed her greatly.

"Yes, I went to see her last week. They look after her so well in that home. All the members of staff are most kindly, but she has deteriorated. She thought I had gone to cut her toenails! I broke the news to her, gently, about her dear friend dying, but I doubt that she really registered it. I'm hoping that she knows, on some level. Rosie will definitely be there to meet her when her time comes." Susie smiled. Phyllis and Rosie were a most unusual duo, but their friendship was set in cement.

"Have you someone on the waiting list, Susie?" Joanna enquired.

"Yes, I do. She's a lady who volunteers at the theatre, as Rosie did and Jean still does. Her name is Elaine. She would be very happy to move in." Susie looked pensive.

"Elaine's a lovely name. I think the group's ready to stretch out its arms again, my friend. Let's do it!" Joanna smiled broadly at Susie and saw her relax.

"You're right. I suppose my reluctance is about upsetting the apple cart, but they're all brave yogis. They'll integrate a newbie with ease." Susie left the bright kitchen feeling enthused.

So it was that Susie put the wheels in motion to take on another elderly resident. Elaine arrived on a Tuesday, carrying her suitcase and a big bunch of roses for the sitting room. The others all greeted her affably. They noted that she had a ready smile and a light step, and that she was obviously delighted to join their community.

Susie laid Elaine's yoga mat in Rosie's space for that afternoon's practice. Jean smiled cheerfully at their new resident, having known her for some while. Marion made a point of patting her shoulder as she passed. Kitty Kara made an appearance for that practice, which was unusual. It felt somehow significant, as though Rosie had sent her feline companion to welcome the newcomer.

Elaine clearly enjoyed the class. She was indeed a smiler. Her face lit up as she joined in with the 'OM Shanti Shanti

Shanti' at the end of the practice, and her eyes twinkled at Susie as she echoed the group chorus of thanks.

"I loved that!" Elaine exuded warmth and good cheer as she turned to Miles. "What a joy to look forward to two classes every day for the rest of my life! I feel truly blessed."

"Well, it's lovely to have you here, Elaine. I'm sure you'll be very happy. We are, as you say, all truly blessed." Miles escorted Elaine to the dining room for supper. He sat with her, as did Jean and Marion. Their table was lively, and as Susie walked through the room she was delighted to see how well the newcomer was being received.

Later that night, Rob heard the whole story from his pretty wife. "I'm sure Rosie is pleased, Rob. She sent Kitty Kara in as a sign. Bless her, she still has time to care about us all. And Elaine is going to be an asset. She sends out very positive vibes." Susie was overflowing with joy and enthusiasm. Every new member to the community reminded her of the reason for the venture.

"I'm very happy that we can offer another elderly yogi a home," Rob declared. "You're spreading the joy, darling, every time you welcome a new student into our family. You're a clever girl." Rob gave Susie a big, warm hug, and she melted into him.

"Well, Yoga," Susie thought, as she relaxed in Rob's arms, practise, intention and joy were all present today. I guess every one of us is a joy ambassador, in our small way."

CHAPTER 22

And Susie asked:

> *"Why is it that in ancient India, where yoga began, the gurus and swamis were all men, but now classes in the West are predominantly female? And why is it that I imagine you to be male, Yoga?"*

Yoga responded, "I noted in your last question that you mentioned two men – the Dalai Lama and Archbishop Tutu. In ancient times, men were attributed with higher intellects and the propensity for wisdom. Women were attributed with compassion and a propensity for nurturing. Their roles in society fed into this stereotype. Men went out into the world to make a living, in order to support their families. Women stayed at home to care for the children and to take care of the domestic duties. It was, initially, the men who practised yoga. In fact, at one time, women were not allowed to practise yoga. It would have been considered unseemly, inappropriate. Besides which, it would not have been considered safe for a single woman to leave home and travel long distances in search of a guru, whereas young men were free to do this. A young man seeking enlightenment would be known as a *chela*, and he would walk for weeks and months to find a teacher. Quite simply, men were teachers because it was possible for them to be so. Perhaps men were also better suited to being solitary, at that time. Women would be inclined to care for their families and their community."

"Yes, that makes sense," Susie agreed. "But why are there currently fewer men than women in yoga classes? Why are young men not still seeking enlightenment?"

"Culture has utterly changed," Yoga explained. "Women are now out there in the world. They're trying to make sense of politics, business and religion. They're questioning and they're seeking knowledge. Many women have discovered that yoga practice will support them as they juggle a career, a family and an ever-changing society. They've become brave and adventurous about travelling. Perhaps they are busy strengthening the masculine side of their natures. Some men find outgoing women threatening. They preferred a time when they could control the women in their families. They feel their authority slipping. Enlightened men see this as progress, however. They embrace the idea of women becoming stronger and taking a more balanced part in the world. In fact, many men are delighted to explore their more feminine side. They stay home to take care of the children, or they work job shares and are home for part of the week. Many men work from home now, and so they are more present with the running of the household. The balance has shifted. Still, however, there are attributes to each sex. Women now search for support and answers.

They search for communities where they can be themselves. They seek emotional release and emotional support from others. A good yoga class offers them that. Men generally are still less inclined to show that need. They feel less able to admit that they need support. They might be more closed, and less able to express their emotions."

"This has been my experience when I've talked to some men about yoga," Susie said. "I do find, though, that when men do brave it and come to a class, they love it. Then they don't leave, and they really don't mind being in the minority. The challenge seems to be to get them there in the first place!"

"Yoga always seeks balance. It will regularise in time. Now, let's move on to the second part of your question. Do you think of me as a man because you've been brought up in a society which is still largely patriarchal? Or do you think of me as a man because you thought the world of your father? Or do you think of me as a man because the ancient yogis, like Mahatma Gandhi for instance, were men?"

"I'm going to give that some thought, Yoga," Susie declared. "I'll get back to you on that one."

Susie took a walk that morning. She always thought better when she was outside and amidst nature. She set up a steady pace, enjoying the feeling of her arms swinging and her feet making contact with the earth. She began to consider the men in her life – her grandfather, her father, her husband, her two sons. Then she thought about her male students, and the elderly yogis in Home from OM. Bernard, Miles and Jimmy were all delightful people. She realised that she liked men. But then, of course, she also liked women!

Susie realised that she had been blessed in her marriage. She and Rob shared a harmonious relationship, one that was based on the yogic values. She observed other couples who bickered constantly. They seemed to exhibit a strong competitive urge towards one another. "That must be really wearing," Susie thought to herself. "I get that there will be tension when one lives with someone all the time, but surely coping skills are needed when stresses occur. I know that I couldn't live in constant conflict."

Susie considered the male and female question again at the end of her evening session at Home from OM. She had observed how it was always Miles who closed the door of the hall when everyone was present. If a window needed opening, it would be Bernard, Miles or Jimmy who would get up to do it. Bernard invariably held the door open for the ladies at the end of the practice. The men enjoyed showing their good manners, and the women enjoyed these small attentions. "Chivalry is not dead yet," Susie thought.

She came back to the query as to why she considered Yoga to be male. "I think it has a lot to do with being protected," she mused. "Still some part of me feels safe with the idea of a strong man looking out for me. But I'm going to do an experiment. I'm going to imagine that Yoga is a woman for the whole of tomorrow. I'll be very interested to see the effect that it has on me."

The next morning Susie was as good as her word. She addressed Yoga and, indeed, visualised Yoga as a goddess. During her early meditation she began to absorb a more nourishing energy. She opened up to gentleness, compassion and love. Yoga embraced her in a very sweet, beautiful and soft way. At the end of her meditation, she thanked Yoga and promised to take this deep, loving energy into her day.

The first person that Susie met in Home from OM that morning was her mother. They hugged fondly, and Susie appreciated the love that she had always received from Marion. When she was a child, she had adored her father, but her mum had always been there for her. She was a permanent in her life. Their connection was truly from heart chakra to heart chakra.

The next person Susie encountered was her long-time friend, Joanna, who was busily preparing the breakfast. Feeding the old yogis nourishing and interesting food was Joanna's mission; one that she accomplished with flair. Watching Joanna cook was to watch love in action, Susie realised.

As she entered the yoga hall, Susie saw Valerie lovingly folding Bernard's meditation shawl. "The feminine energy of caring is very present here this morning," Susie thought, with a private grin.

The practice that morning referenced *bhakti yoga*: the yoga of love and devotion. They began their class with three resounding 'OM's. Susie certainly could have been described as a *bhakta*, a devotee. She ran the home from a place of love, and she had devoted her entire career to Brahman, the Supreme Being. They chanted in meditation, using a jolly tune as they sang 'OM Namah Shivaya'. One translation for this Sanskrit chant is 'I surrender to love'.

Susie observed that both the men and the women enjoyed the chanting. Shiva is, of course, a Hindu god. He is most definitely male, and is said to destroy and cleanse by the means of fire. Susie realised that she had a statue of

Shiva in the home. They also had Ganesh and Krishna. All of these are male. She made a mental note to seek a statue of Lakshmi, the goddess of wealth, fortune and prosperity. Lakshmi is the wife and Shakti energy of Vishnu. Then her eye fell on a beautiful crystal lotus flower on the window-sill of the yoga hall. "Of course," she thought, "the lotus flower brings the softness, the femininity to mind."

Susie held the feminine aspect of Yoga in her heart all day long. She noticed how she picked up on every gentle gesture of love in the yoga community. Even the house cat, Kitty Kara, was sweetly sharing her affections amongst the old yogis. "This has been a most interesting experiment, Yoga," Susie admitted as she snuggled down in bed that night. "I've loved working with you as a feminine entity. And, of course, I have realised that you are a perfect combination of the male and the female. It's simply my perception that alters. Thank you for that lesson! You knew that I would get there eventually. So the answer to the question that began this experiment is that male energy is strong and necessary, female energy is gentle and necessary. The beauty of yoga is the way that it takes both strengths and brings balance to them. I might just think of you as male one day, and then think of you as female the next day. That will bring balance to my teaching." Susie fell asleep with that thought.

CHAPTER 23

And Susie asked:

"When I chose to become a yoga teacher, was that my decision or yours? And which one of us decided to create an old yogis' home?"

Elaine, the new resident in Home from OM, had settled in really well. She had green fingers and had immediately volunteered to help make Rosie's memorial garden with Jamila. Currently, they were creating a rockery and had filled it with the purple shades of aubretia and campanula. They had added a really pretty pink saxifrage for later in the season. Elaine and Jamila became firm friends.

Susie happened on Elaine one day sitting on a bench in the garden. The sweet lady was in tears. "Hello, Elaine," Susie said softly. "Anything I can do to help?"

Elaine looked up at Susie and smiled through the tears. "No thank you, my love," she replied, with a catch in her voice. "I'm being silly. It's just that I'm so happy to be here. I was just suddenly overcome with emotion at the thought of how lucky I am. Everyone has been so kind and welcoming. This community is so much more than I expected."

Susie was relieved. "Oh, that's lovely," she said, with a big smile. "But you know, Elaine, it's a two-way street. You've fitted in with such grace. You have a beautiful, light energy, which we all appreciate."

Elaine's tears began to flow again, but they were happy tears. "I just feel so privileged," she blurted out, "this has been the best decision of my life."

Susie gave Elaine a hug and left her to her thoughts.

"Now, Yoga," Susie asked in her mind, "did Elaine decide to join us here, or did you lead her footsteps?"

"You may be over-complicating things, Susie," was the infuriating reply. "Does it matter, when the end result is the same?"

"Yes, Yoga," Susie countered. "It matters to me!"

Jane had requested a meeting with Rob and Susie that evening. She had a few innovations to suggest. Jane had proved to be an exceptional manager for the home. She was bright, efficient and caring. Seated in the office when they arrived, Jane was wearing a friendly grin on her attractive face. "Thanks for coming," she began. "How are you both?"

When the pleasantries were over, Jane launched into some new ideas that she had come up with. "I do hope that you don't think I'm being pushy, but sometimes I can see some shortcuts that might prove helpful." Jane's ideas were all sensible and were mostly concerned with the laundry and the house rota. Rob and Susie were very happy to consider them, and most of them were agreed immediately.

At the end of the meeting, Rob thanked their manager warmly. "How would we cope without you, Jane?" he enquired. "You run our little establishment so efficiently, and we do appreciate you."

Jane smiled widely. "I love my job here, Rob, it's literally a joy to come to work. What a difference it makes working somewhere when you so applaud the intention of the place."

"I'd like to thank you so very much for making Elaine welcome too, Jane," Susie enthused. "We have a lovely team of yogis, but the home only works because of those, like you, who support them."

It did seem to Susie, walking home hand in hand with her husband, that everyone involved in Home from OM had been sent there from a higher source. Jane was right when she mentioned 'intention'. Susie knew with every cell in her body that the old yogis' home was fulfilling a deep need in society.

"You're right, of course, Yoga," she admitted later, as she cleaned her teeth. "I am over-complicating things. When I return to the original meaning of the word 'yoga' – union – it becomes absolutely clear to me that it's impossible to separate out who has determined what. And as long as we're all moving in the right direction, it doesn't matter a jot. I guess I rather like the idea that you and I are both making my decisions!"

"Just follow the love in your heart, Susie," Yoga replied. "All is well."

CHAPTER 24

And Susie asked:

"But why me?"

The last question had stayed in Susie's mind and now she wanted to satisfy another query. Why had Yoga chosen her for this mission? There were so many fine yoga teachers out in the world, after all.

"When we sat around a virtual table in Spirit World to discuss your next incarnation, Susie, you emphasised that you wanted to make a difference. You wanted to take yoga to the world in a way that would be readily understood but, more than that, you insisted that you wanted to show a way of really helping mankind. There's a huge challenge facing all peoples right now, and that is how to cope with the numbers of elderly. An idea was embraced. It's not a new idea, of course, but it's one that can make a profound difference."

"That makes sense, Yoga," Susie agreed. "I still have that driving desire to change the world, one breath at a time."

This interaction filled Susie with determination. She found it immensely comforting that she was following her life's plan. These dialogues with Yoga kept her focussed.

Max and Megan were planning to visit for the weekend. Max had not forgotten his promise to do some heavy work for Rosie's memorial garden. Jamila and Elaine were looking forward to completing their task, and were considering a small ceremony of remembrance.

"There are a few more plants I'd like to purchase at the garden centre, Elaine," Jamila mentioned one day at lunch. "Are you free to come this afternoon?"

"Yes, I'd like that," Elaine was quick to agree to the plan. "What time do you have in mind?"

"I was thinking of about two thirty. Then we'll have time for a good mooch and be back in plenty of time to get ready for yoga." Jamila smiled at her new friend. The two ladies left very happily in Jamila's car, spent a most enjoyable time browsing the rows of colourful plants on offer, and returned delighted with their selections.

"We're all ready for the weekend, Susie," Jamila told their teacher later. "Now don't sidetrack Max with talk of the impending wedding! We need his youthful enthusiasm in the garden."

Susie laughed. "Megan will no doubt update me as you all dig and plant. Do you think you'll be ready for the little remembrance ritual on Sunday afternoon, Jamila?"

"That's the plan," Jamila replied. "We're going to put some of Rosie's crystals in place and, hopefully, we can gather everyone together. Do you think Bernard would read the poem again from the funeral?"

"That would be lovely," Susie agreed, "and I'm sure he would. Let's plan it for three o'clock and anyone who would like to can say a few words."

Saturday morning was a bustling time in the garden. Elaine and Jamila recruited Rob and Miles as well as Max. Susie, down the road with Megan, could hear the laughter as the guys teased one another. "Thank goodness for glorious weather, Megan," said Susie fondly to her daughter-in-law-to-be. "If only we could order this for the wedding!"

"Actually, Susie, we're beginning to get down to the nitty-gritty of the arrangements now. My mum and dad have booked their local church for the wedding, which will be just lovely, and we had provisionally booked a venue for the reception. But we're having a rethink. We'd very much like everyone from Home from OM to come, and now we're wondering if it's too far for them all to travel. I know it's only forty miles, but it will make it a long day for them. Do you fancy having the reception here instead?" Megan grinned at Susie, endeavouring to gauge her reaction.

"Wow! What a fantastic notion," Susie enthused. "We'd love it! Are you thinking of hiring a marquee? But what about your family, Megan, will your parents mind the drive?"

"No, they're up for it. We're thinking of hiring a bus to bring us all. Wouldn't that be fun? And all the oldies would get such a thrill out of wearing their hats and being part of the celebrations."

"And, after today, the garden is going to be even prettier for the occasion. I'm excited, Megan. You are such a delight!"

Susie and Megan shared a warm hug, while both their minds turned to imagining the special day.

Rob and Max were delighted to hear that all had been agreed. Now they would have to get busy finding caterers and organising the flowers.

"So," Susie murmured to Yoga later that night, "I come up with a plan in Spirit World to make a difference, and now my son is celebrating his nuptials at Home from OM. All of us will be uniting and remembering that union is the meaning of the word 'yoga'. Yes, this splendid occasion will infuse our establishment with even more love. I'm blessed, and I'm even more grateful that it's me that has been chosen for this mission. Thank you, Yoga."

Rosie would have loved her memorial garden. She would have loved the ceremony which took place to remember her. Even her furry friend, Kitty Kara, put in an appearance on Sunday afternoon. She was attracted by the gathering of all her favourite people, and rubbed around their ankles as they stood, heads bowed. Her purrs accompanied the many kind words that were spoken. Perhaps Jamila's quote was the most poignant: "The love in your heart was not put there to stay. Love is not love until you give it away. We love you, Rosie."

CHAPTER 25

And Susie asked:

"How many times have I reincarnated as a yoga teacher?"

"Three," was the curt reply.
"And would it be useful for me to know about those other lives?"

"No need," Yoga responded.

"Is there no need because it wouldn't shed light on my current life, or no need because dwelling on the past is not helpful?" Susie looked puzzled.

"On both counts – there's no need." Yoga was infuriatingly terse this morning!

Susie reached the conclusion that Yoga was busy with important matters. She would go on considering this for herself.

Marion was the first person that she met on entering the home that morning. They shared a hug but did not speak. Silence was always observed before the early morning meditation.

Susie took them through three rounds of Salutation to the Sun during the hatha yoga part of the class. Jimmy was invariably a beat behind the others in all the movements, but Jamila's lithe body was so graceful in the postures that Julia couldn't help but be distracted. "I must tell her what an inspiration she is," Julia determined. Bernard and Valerie managed to be in complete unison, and Susie grinned appreciatively at them.

At the end of the practice, they all felt lighter and well-stretched. Having chanted 'OM Shanti Shanti Shanti', they all moved towards the dining room for breakfast. The topic of conversation for some of the yogis was the upcoming wedding. "We did a great present for the engagement," Jean began, "but what shall we come up with for a wedding present?"

Maureen had been considering the same question. "I was thinking of perhaps something frivolous. Would a hammock for the garden be terribly silly?" Maureen looked embarrassed. She was still a nervous lady and somewhat tentative, even after her years with the community. To her surprise, everyone loved the idea. "That strikes just the right note," Jean enthused.

"I love that idea," Valerie agreed.

Bernard remembered spending time in a hammock in India. "They used to hang them between the coconut trees," he said. "I was warned that you have to move very fast if a coconut leaves the branch, because travelling at speed it could, of course, kill you. Apparently, it's ten times more likely that you'll be killed by a coconut than a shark!"

Miles grinned, "I think they'll be pretty safe hanging the hammock between apple trees," he mused, "although even an apple could give you a black eye. We're going to need a health and safety warning on the gift!"

"Oh, I feel a poem coming on!" laughed Pam. "We could turn this into a brilliant bit of irony! You know how much Max and Megan enjoy tongue-in-cheek humour."

Valerie and Marion had arranged a shopping trip to buy their outfits for the big day. They planned to go to Chichester. "Will you wear a sari, Jamila?" Marion asked her.

"Oh, yes, I certainly will," Jamila said. "Actually, I've been wondering whether Susie might like to wear a sari, too."

"What a gorgeous idea," Valerie looked thrilled. "Wouldn't Susie look fabulous. I was asking Bernard the other day if the Indian ladies minded westerners wearing their stunning clothes. He said no, and that actually they really enjoy it. They take it as a compliment."

"That's right," Jamila agreed. "And with Susie's colouring and slim figure she would look stunning. I'll see what she says."

Susie loved the idea, but said that she must first check with Megan and her mother. She didn't want to upstage either of them, but then perhaps wearing a sari would mean that she would be sufficiently different not to cause any competition.

"I wonder if I've been Indian in a former life," Susie mused later that day. "And I wonder if I've been a man in India?" She remembered Yoga's statement that there was 'no need' to know about her former lives, but it was still fun to speculate!

CHAPTER 26

And Susie asked:

"So we have eleven old yogis in our home. Did they enter a commitment with one another in Spirit World? Did they agree to spend their final years together in this incarnation?"

Susie found this to be a natural follow-up to her last question.

Yoga replied to the query immediately. "Yes, of course they did."

"How fascinating is that?" Susie thought. She observed her oldies even more closely that day. "So, on a soul level, Valerie knew that she would meet her Prince Charming here in the home. And Rosie and Phyllis knew that they would be soulmates. Even the unconditional love that Maureen received from dear Alice was prearranged."

There was something wonderfully liberating about the idea that the universe was colluding with them all to bring their plans and lessons into being. "I knew that I had chosen my parents, my husband and my children in Spirit World,"

Susie commented to Yoga, "but I guess I hadn't taken that further step. So, when we moved next to Alice and Ted, we were simply following a larger plan. I read once that each one of us works on our corner of the patchwork quilt, but only God, or Brahman, can see the whole."

"That's precisely right, Susie," Yoga agreed. "This is the essence of Krishna's teaching to Arjuna in the *Bhagavad Gita*. He instructs Arjuna to follow his path and to trust. All human beings are given free will, but they have already discussed what they hope to achieve in this lifetime. It's helpful to remember to trust in your process when facing difficult times."

Susie smiled. "Yes, that's a really cheering thought."

The yoga classes that day were themed on trust. Susie peppered them with the well-loved statement: 'All is well and all shall be well'. She observed that her old yogis fretted less than younger folk. They had reached a point in their lives where they could trust and surrender to the inevitable. She was learning, too. She was learning that not only 'what would be would be', but that 'what would be was meant to be'.

That evening, Rob had organised a quiz in the lounge for the residents. The questions would be partially yoga-oriented and partially concerned with current news items. Susie was there to support, but had ample time to observe her students. They split into three teams. Julia had suggested that each of the men should head up a team, so Bernard presided over Valerie and Marion, while Miles teamed up with Jamila, Elaine and Maureen. This left Jimmy captaining the team of Pam, Jean and Julia.

Susie thoroughly enjoyed watching how the teams interacted. The idea that this group of people had chosen to spend their golden years with one another fascinated her. "So," thought Susie, "just as yoga works on all levels, so does spiritual choice. These lovely people chose to spend their retirement together on the physical level, on the mental level and on the spiritual level. No wonder that many of them expressed the idea that it felt like 'coming home' when they joined Home from OM. They were tuning into their predestination. They could feel the 'rightness' of their decision."

Just at that moment a roar of laughter erupted from Jimmy's team. Susie put her ruminations to one side and fully engaged with proceedings.

CHAPTER 27

And Susie asked:

"I fully understand now that our community has been agreed and planned in advance. However, have our elderly yogis agreed to an experiment? Are we colluding to offer them an alternative world, or an escape from the world?"

The residents of the home led a gentle life. They were free to participate in any aspect of the running of the home that they chose and they had become a large and loving family. Susie and Rob ensured that the home abided by the yoga philosophies, so it was run on principles that ensured healthy eating, healthy exercise, and healthy interaction. There was always something to look forward to, and right now much of the talk was about Max and Megan's fast approaching nuptials.

When the big day arrived, no-one was surprised that the weather was sunny and mild. Susie had decided, after discussion with Megan and her mother, to wear an Indian salwar kameez. The material was exquisite and the colours worked with the theme of the wedding outfits, which was all about sweet peas. As she explained to her mum, Marion, "I'd love to wear a sari, as Jamila suggested, but I think I'll be more comfortable this way. The trousers and top of a salwar kameez are so practical, and I can wear the chumni, the scarf, for the wedding service and the photographs, then fold it away later for the dancing."

Rob and Susie arrived at the church in good time. Toby looked so smart as he greeted them. Being tall, he looked splendid in a grey suit complete with tails. He had sweet peas in his buttonhole and the shiniest black shoes ever. "Wow! You look gorgeous!" Susie proudly exclaimed. "Your shoes are so shiny!"

"Wait till you see Max's," Toby laughed. "He's polished the bottoms as well, so that when he kneels, they'll look amazing!"

Toby fastened a buttonhole arrangement of sweet peas in to his father's grey suit, and handed a tiny and immaculate bouquet to his mum. "Megan says that this fastens to your clutch bag," Toby grinned. "I'm learning to do precisely what Megan decrees. She will not to be crossed or teased over this wedding!"

"That's quite right," Rob grinned back at him. "I learnt this at our wedding – never challenge the bride!"

Toby was then called away, and Rob and Susie took their places in the church. Megan's mother had done a beautiful job of decking out the church with bouquets of sweet peas. Their fragrance subtly filled the space. Max came to hug his parents, looking immaculate and achingly handsome. Susie's eyes filled with tears and, seeing this, he gave her an extra squeeze.

The church was filling up nicely, and Rob and Susie picked out some of Max's friends from university. Toby escorted Megan's mother up the aisle, and seated her carefully. She looked stunning in a dress and jacket of pink, which toned beautifully with her sweet pea corsage. Her hat was a triumph of sophistication, and good taste. Susie smiled across at her and mouthed, "You look amazing!"

The ushers having seated all the guests, and the organ music filling the church, Max waited beside his twin brother somewhat nervously. He needn't have worried. His bride arrived on time, gently leaning on her father's arm. It will surprise no-one to know that she was the most beautiful bride ever! She had elected to wear her mother's wedding dress. It was ivory lace and the simplicity of its cut showed Megan's figure off to full advantage. The bride's bouquet was simple and her hair natural; her biggest adornment was her smile, which lit up the building. Max thought that she floated with an ethereal grace, as he turned to watch her process up the aisle.

The wedding ceremony was charming. The couple said their vows clearly and with conviction. The two little bridesmaids, one in lilac and one in tangerine, carried baskets of sweet peas. To everyone's relief (particularly the grown-up bridesmaid), they were so awed by the solemn atmosphere that they behaved impeccably.

The bells rang gloriously as the wedding party emerged from the church, and the photographs taken that day reflected the joy of the occasion.

Eventually, Toby, taking his role as best man very seriously, ushered folk towards the bus which would take them to Home from OM for the reception. Some had elected to drive themselves the forty miles, but those who entered the bus were in for a treat. It was decked out with balloons in sweet pea colours, and the music the happy couple had chosen ensured an upbeat atmosphere. The journey passed in a spirit of great jollity.

Meanwhile, Joanna and Jane had been busy at the home. The atmosphere and tension was building as the bus approached, and they were eager to have everything ready. The caterers had excelled themselves and the marquee was indeed a place of enchantment. Sweet peas, of course, decorated each table. The old yogis had dressed with care. No way were they going to let Rob and Susie down! Jamila's sari gave the group a splash of colour as they gathered to wait for the bus. The silk of the material was in autumn colours – russet and gold – which enhanced Jamila's Indian beauty.

Of course the couple were liberally dowsed with rose petals when they emerged from their jolly transport! And of course the old yogis hugged them both with vigour! All were welcomed and rounded up, and a sea of people moved into the marquee. There they found their seats, and were supplied with champagne or orange juice.

The food for the celebration was both well-presented and well-received. Toby sipped his wine with restraint, not wanting to mar the quality of his best man's speech. One of Max's university friends, Spencer, visited each table and set up a sweepstake on how long Toby's speech would be!

When the moment arrived, Toby's nerves evaporated and he delivered a hilarious string of anecdotes concerning his brother. Rob and Susie were familiar with most of these stories, but even they were surprised by the story of the plum tree. It seemed that the twins decided to raid a plum tree at the other end of the village. They were about nine at the time and, being twins, were always ready to egg one another on. They climbed the tree successfully, perched on the branches and began to devour the golden plums. Unfortunately, Max became a little over-ambitious and inched along a rather less robust branch to reach the 'most awesome plums'. The branch gave way, and Max landed heavily, narrowly missing the rabbit hutch on the lawn. The householder was alerted by the noise, and Toby just managed to descend from his perch and drag his limping twin from the scene. On reaching the safety of home, they spent half an hour concocting a believable story to explain to their parents where Max's rather large bruises had come from! It amused Rob and Susie to realise why the boys had always gone into fits of giggles whenever the first plums of the season appeared in the fruit bowl. They had put it down to a silly poem which the boys would recite to cover their mirth. The rhyming of 'plum' with 'bum' had disguised the real reason for the irrepressible laughter!

Toby certainly had skill as a public speaker and Max was thoroughly, but kindly, teased. To the amusement of all the old yogis, Miles won the sweepstake. His guess of twenty-two minutes was spot on. Miles determined to donate the money to the Indian ashram and orphanage which they supported.

After the completion of the speeches, the cake was cut and shared. Then a tidy up of the tables allowed space for dancing. The live band was excellent and, to everyone's delight, the young married couple had rehearsed a Bollywood number for their first dance. The whole place erupted with rapturous applause and Toby confided to his mother, "Even I didn't know about that!"

Rob waited for his opportunity to dance with his beautiful new daughter-in-law and to congratulate her on making the day such a joy. Max danced with his mother, his mother-in-law and with his grandmother, Marion. She was so proud that she looked fit to burst! Meanwhile, Jimmy, Bernard and Miles spread themselves gallantly amongst the ladies from 'Home for OM'.

Eventually, the band began to play music to suit the younger folk, and the oldies retired to the garden to chat. "Well, Jamila," said Jean, "I'm afraid Max didn't arrive on an elephant, but how did this very English wedding shape up for you?"

Jamila laughed. "I do remember the joke that we had about Bernard arriving on an elephant to marry Valerie," she replied, "but the Bollywood dance was just the right nod to India and yoga. I loved it! What a stunning couple they are."

Valerie agreed and added, "Susie looks fantastic in her Indian outfit, too. I've had the best time. Wasn't it kind of the young people to organise the reception here? Now we oldies can retire to our beds just when we're ready."

Many hours later, as they made their way down the road to their house, it was clear to Susie that the old folk had enjoyed themselves just as much as the young. Her heart had made a little leap as she watched Toby flirting with Megan's cousin, Sophie. The vivacious brunette had captured his interest from the moment that they were introduced. "Who knows," Susie mused, "there might be another wedding before too long!"

The way the residents of the yoga home had interacted with each other, and with the other guests, convinced Susie that their connection was deep-rooted. "As always, Yoga, you're right," she admitted as she fell exhausted into her bed. "A contract was surely made between all of the old yogis in Spirit World. They fill me with admiration. They love one another and they love all of us. What a day this has been! It's truly been a celebration of love and connection. Right now I don't care whether we've created an escape from the world or simply an alternative world. I'll think about it tomorrow."

CHAPTER 28

And Susie asked:

"What is a yoga teacher, anyway?"

A few days later, Susie was given the opportunity to consider her previous question whilst talking to a non-yogi. Megan's mother, Amanda, had phoned to chat about the wedding. "I heard briefly from Megan and Max," she chuckled. "They're having a brilliant time in La Gomera. Megan says that it is extraordinarily peaceful. They've done lots of walking and swimming. It sounds like the perfect honeymoon."

"Yes, and they really do deserve a break. They were so thoughtful with all the details for the wedding that everyone had a marvellous time. We saw a photo that they'd posted up on Facebook. They both looked so well and happy."

"James and I were talking about your elderly residents, Susie," Amanda continued. "They're all so lovely and so sociable. They're really an advert for living out your retirement in a yoga community. We loved meeting them."

Susie was thrilled to think that Amanda and her husband, James, appreciated how special her old yogis were.

"I've been debating whether we give them an alternative world here in Home from OM or an escape from the real world," Susie admitted.

"Oh, the former is definitely the case," Amanda replied. "They couldn't have interacted so beautifully with all the wedding guests if they had been closeted away from the world. They just seem to be able to express their full potential. It's as though yoga practice and living in the yoga home has given them permission to show their love and positivity. They really manifest how we could all live if we practised goodness. It's convinced me, Susie – I'm looking for a local yoga class!"

Susie laughed. "That's excellent! We have a new recruit! And if and when Megan and Max have our grandchildren, they'll have two super supple grandmothers to run around after them!"

"And that is to say nothing of a bunch of old yogis to spoil and inspire them! Oh, and by the way, we loved that they bought Megan and Max a hammock! What a fun gift. And the poem that accompanied it was truly inspired. Megan's going to frame it."

Susie was delighted with her phone call with Amanda. It was good to hear from someone who was not directly involved with the home that she was indeed on the right path. It wasn't until the afternoon class that she received a reply from Yoga on her current question. During the long relaxation Yoga said, "A yoga teacher is simply a guide. Through teaching and example, the yoga teacher gives her students techniques for holistic living."

"I like that definition, Yoga," Susie said. "Now tell me, how does teaching yoga differ from teaching any other subject?"

"In some ways teaching any subject requires the same skills. Firstly, it's essential that the teacher is motivated to impart knowledge in an easily digested form. Secondly, they need to like people and to have good people skills. Thirdly, they need to have a solid grasp of their subject matter. But, and this is quite a big but, teaching yoga is all about love. It takes a big heart to share love with all the students in a class; it takes great patience to hold the class in the healing space; and it takes a pure spirit to channel the truest essence of the yoga message. In short, a yoga teacher has to have a little bit of magic in their soul!"

"Gosh," Susie exclaimed, mentally, "that makes me feel very humble, Yoga. I do know that sometimes it just feels right. It feels as though we're all in accord, and embraced by a bubble of love. The atmosphere in the room, on occasions, is awesome."

"Yes, and of course, you are not on your own as a yoga teacher. Your spirit guides, your guardian angels and the archangels all look out for you. I am there to assist," Yoga added.

"I do feel that," Susie admitted, "and I'm really grateful. Whenever I start the class with 'Namaste' I believe that the gesture of Anjali Mudra requests that the students be given what they need at that moment. After all these years of teaching yoga, it still feels like a real privilege. It's the best job in the world!"

Susie glowed at the end of that practice. The glow stayed with her and Rob noticed it as they sat to eat supper together. "You're looking particularly beautiful today, darling," he said. "You grow lovelier and more serene all the time. Had a good day?"

"Yes, I have," Susie replied with enthusiasm, "and thank you, kind sir, for the compliment! I had a lovely chat with Amanda earlier. She and I will have such fun being grandmothers, when the time comes!"

Rob grinned, "No, it's not possible! You're nowhere near old enough to be a grandmother!"

"Well it will be a rite of passage," Susie admitted. "But we liked the whole parenting thing, so I'm convinced we'll love grand-parenting."

"Let's cross that bridge when we come to it," Rob said. "I'm confident that, with good-looking parents like Megan and Max, they'll be gorgeous kids!"

"While we're chatting Rob," Susie continued, "how would you define a yoga teacher?"

"You, sweetheart, are the personification of a yoga teacher," Rob said with a twinkle. "Folk only need to know you for a very short time before they realise that yoga is all about love. You show that in the way that you teach and the way that you live."

"That's very sweet, very flattering and very loyal, my love, but it's not specific enough. Now, think about it, and give me a definition." Susie looked serious, and Rob obeyed the instruction.

"Okay, I've given the matter some thought: 'A yoga teacher is one who imparts the ancient philosophy of yoga by demonstrating its tools and techniques to achieve health and well-being'," Rob decreed.

"That's good. Thank you, Rob." Susie reached up and kissed her husband.

Her question wasn't totally answered in her mind, though, and Susie determined to ask everyone possible for their personal definition. On the following day, she sought out Marion.

"Hi, Mum," she began, having tracked her mother down in the sitting room, "I have a question for you. Please could you give me your definition of a yoga teacher?"

Marion thought for a moment and then declared, "'A yoga teacher shares good practice with her students. She teaches them to be aware and to be mindful.' Is that the sort of thing that you're looking for, Susie?"

Susie was busy scribbling down her mother's words. "Just the ticket – thanks Mum," she said. Then she spotted Jamila in the garden talking to Bernard. "I'm off to collect two more definitions, Mum. Thank you for yours."

Marion was left wondering whether her daughter was planning to embark on a new career. Was she going to write a book? Nothing would surprise Marion. Susie had boundless energy.

"Jamila, Bernard," Susie called, as she approached them. "Sorry to interrupt, but could I ask you both to come up with a definition of a yoga teacher?"

"Let's see," Bernard said with a frown. "Yoga is a huge subject and each yoga teacher brings a different emphasis to their classes. I would say that: 'A yoga teacher lives the yoga way of life. Through example they bring their students into balance.'"

Susie jotted this down, and then Jamila said, "I agree with Bernard. That's a good definition, but I'm going to go with: 'A yoga teacher drip feeds words of wisdom to her students with the intention of increasing their physical, mental, emotional and spiritual health.' That's what I feel is my plan, anyway."

"That's great. Thank you both very much. It's fascinating how many different answers I'm getting!" Susie laughed.

Next Susie headed for the kitchen. She had decided it would be fun to ask Joanna and Jane. Joanna had been practising yoga for a long time, but Jane, although she managed the yoga home, had never been to a class.

"Hi, lovely ladies," she began, "I'm doing a bit of market research. How would you define a yoga teacher?"

Joanna looked amused. "Are you doubting your path, Susie?" she laughed. "I would have come to you with that query!"

"No, it's just become very interesting to hear other people's opinion on this," Susie said. "I'm gathering the answers, but I'm not quite sure how I shall use them yet."

"I would say: 'A yoga teacher has a responsibility to share peace, joy, love and harmony with her or his students.' How does that sound?" Joanna smiled at her friend.

"That's great. All the definitions are different. I'm loving this research! Now, let's turn to a non-yogi. How would you define a yoga teacher, Jane?" Susie turned her gaze on her very efficient manager.

"You're putting me on the spot here, Susie," Jane laughed, "but I'm going to approach this from my observations. 'A yoga teacher provides an oasis of calm. A yoga teacher provides time to reflect. A yoga teacher offers a healing space.' How did I do?"

"You did really well. I'm inclined to think that gathering these definitions is going to be a longer job than I expected! Thank you both very much."

Susie left the kitchen in search of more opinions.

Maureen shyly observed how important it was to her that the yoga teacher used contraindications. She felt safe in Susie's hands, and trusted that she was following instructions which would keep her free from risk.

Miles stated that: 'A yoga teacher is one who creates a rhythm and a flow in the practices', while Valerie asserted: 'A yoga teacher is someone who imparts the wisdom of yoga with verve and enthusiasm'.

The latest recruit to the home, Elaine, maintained that: 'A yoga teacher is in a unique position to offer loving support as their students gain in health and happiness'.

Susie squirrelled away all of these definitions and began to analyse her own take on 'What is a yoga teacher, anyway?' She knew in her heart that teaching yoga was a great privilege. She knew that it had always been her path. She knew with every part of her being that yoga enriched her on every level. Susie harboured a vague idea that she might embroider some of these definitions on to a wall hanging for either Home from OM or Wellness Within – her yoga and health centre. But, meanwhile, she smiled to think of what fun it had been to ask everyone their opinions. She had another idea forming in her mind. "How about if I ask each of the old yogis to come up with a question for you, Yoga?" she pondered.

"I think that's an exceptionally good notion, Susie," Yoga replied. "Now tell me, what are you as a yoga teacher?"

"I've been exploring various definitions, Yoga," Susie admitted, "and now you've put a different slant on it! What am I as a yoga teacher…? Well, I'm an ambassador for a more balanced way of life. By teaching others to work with their bodies, minds, emotions, breath and inner spirit, I spread yoga's eternal message of health, happiness and fulfilment."

"That's excellent," Yoga responded. "Know yourself, Susie, and be true to yourself always."

Susie was keen to action her plan to give the residents of the home an opportunity to lodge questions with Yoga. She mentioned it at the end of their evening practice the very next day. "Think about it," she suggested, "then write down your queries and we'll offer them to our great authority, Yoga himself."

Some of the students looked a little bemused. Bernard looked intrigued, while Jamila smiled with glee. "This is going to be fun," Susie thought. "I'm fascinated to see what they come up with!"

- PART THREE -

YOGIS POSE QUESTIONS

CHAPTER 29

And Bernard asked:

"Will yoga ever win in the good versus evil discussion?"

Susie received Bernard's question first of all. He readily understood that she perceived yoga as a person, as a mentor and guide. Susie relayed Bernard's query to Yoga during their early morning long relaxation. "Now I know that you already understand what is in Bernard's mind and in his heart, Yoga, but I'll give this process a procedure. Please would you consider: 'Will yoga ever win in the good versus evil discussion?' I'm fascinated to hear your response."

"Bernard is a sincere and committed yogi," Yoga began, "and this is a very valid question. I shall formulate my answer and deliver it to you later."

Susie was amused to hear the other residents discussing their questions as she walked through the dining room during breakfast. Maureen looked confused and confided to Julia, "I'm a little unsure about this. Can I ask something very personal, do you think?"

"Certainly you can," Julia replied firmly. "I see this as an opportunity for us all to express a deeply held enquiry. In fact it needs to be something personal."

Maureen looked reassured.

"Have you written yours, Jamila?" Elaine enquired.

"Yes, I have," Jamila replied quickly. "What about you, Jean?"

"I'm still deliberating," Jean admitted. "It's great fun, though. It turns our mindset around. We're so accustomed to Susie answering our unspoken queries in that rather magical way of hers. You know how sometimes you feel that she's talking directly to you in the class? It's as though the whole practice has been designed with you in mind. Well, this puts the responsibility back on us. And, absurd as it sounds, it kind of makes me feel that a higher authority is more available to me."

Jamila nodded in agreement. Elaine looked pensive. "As the newest recruit to your yoga family," she said, "I shall wait till all the other questions have been asked before submitting mine."

Susie was very pleased with the reaction from the elderly residents. They never failed to impress! She had planned to clean Wellness Within that morning. Her yoga studio and health centre had been up and running for a year now. She fully recognised how blessed she was to have this establishment right next door to her home. It was unusual for it not to be buzzing with activity, so Susie took advantage of the quiet time to survey the hall. It was a beautiful, south-facing room that was often bathed in sunshine. The views from the windows were pleasing. When they turned to do Salute to the Moon, the students could see beautiful cherry trees in full bloom, in the spring, and horses grazing in a distant paddock. The village was a quiet place to live and, as Susie paused to listen, she could only hear the song of a blackbird and the distant hum of a lawn mower.

Having hoovered and polished the floor, Susie turned her attention to the bathrooms. She kept in mind *saucha*, which was one of the *niyamas*: the 'do's' of Patanjali's *Eight Limbs*. *Saucha* means 'cleanliness' or 'purification'. There is an order, a neatness, to yoga practice and that is reflected in the space used for practice.

Having finished attending to the hall, Susie turned her attention to the treatment rooms. These were upstairs and were kept neat by the various therapists who rented them for their clients. Susie hummed as she worked, ever mindful that her energy needed to be gentle and kind. She would be leaving an energy imprint on these healing spaces.

Returning home for lunch some time later, Susie discovered Rob in the study looking over the books. "Oh dear," she grinned, "am I due for a lecture on the finances of the home?"

"No, my love, it's actually all looking pretty healthy right now. Are you going to make a sandwich? I'll join you if you are." Rob was happy to leave his desk and they spent a most pleasant hour together eating and chatting.

Later on, at the beginning of the evening yoga session at Home from OM, Susie read out Bernard's question. The group of yogis were able to consider it themselves as the practice unfolded. As Susie had anticipated, Yoga had a reply for him during the long relaxation.

"Please tell Bernard that yoga *is* winning. When you look at the yin and yang symbol, you realise that there is a balance in all things. There is a balance between right and left, a balance between upper and lower, a balance between masculine and feminine, and a balance between good and evil. Yoga practice is all about bringing folk into balance. Through aeons of time, yoga has laboured to keep the belief in goodness and love alive. This has not been in vain. All energies are currently becoming finer, that is to say both the energies of goodness and the energies of evil. Right at this moment a revolution is occurring in this world. Negativity is rising to the surface. We are being made very aware of evil, but with that awareness comes the means to overcome it. When we see fully, we can find a solution. Yoga, in addition to right-thinking religions, philosophers, teachers and the whole body of good people on the planet, will ensure that benevolence is dominant. All energies are becoming finer. We are ascending. Yes, please tell Bernard that yoga is winning. On a purely practical level, do look at how the message of yoga is spreading in the West. There will soon be more retirement communities such as yours, Susie. You can rest assured about that."

Susie felt reassured by Yoga's comments, and she was delighted to relay them to Bernard at the end of the class. The other students listened attentively. This was proving to be a most interesting venture!

CHAPTER 30

And Jamila asked:

"Why doesn't everyone practise yoga?"

Susie read out Jamila's question the following afternoon, as that procedure had worked well the previous day. Jamila smiled at her fellow residents as they all chuckled. How many other yoga teachers must ask themselves this question on a daily basis!

During the long relaxation, Susie relayed this query to Yoga. His reply was prompt.

"It stretches our imagination, when we believe strongly in the philosophy and wisdom of yoga practice, to understand why everyone does not regularly attend classes," Yoga began, "but it is a lot to do with karma. All folk set up their present lifetime to work out past karmic patterns and to learn their lessons. They need to process those lessons in the appropriate way. As yogis ourselves, we believe that yoga will speed up the work. We believe that yoga brings us into balance, hastens our realisations, and brings us closer to Brahman. However, each soul must find its own path to bliss or *samadhi*. We can't be so arrogant as to inflict our beliefs on others. They must make their own choices. I do realise that this question comes from a yoga teacher, through a yoga teacher, and that it's partially tongue in cheek. All I can add is that we in Spirit World are all delighted with the progress that our representatives are making on Earth. Please ask Jamila to keep on keeping on."

Jamila was very pleased with this answer. It set up a lively discussion over dinner. Valerie was firmly of the opinion that yoga should be mandatory in all schools. Bernard's granddaughter, Charlotte, was fortunate to have a yoga teacher visiting her school each week. "We must begin with the next generation," Valerie insisted. "If we can start them off young, they'll grow up quite naturally understanding the yogic values. I read once that all old peoples' homes should be built opposite an orphanage. Can't you just see the wisdom of that? Suppose our yoga community was involved with less privileged children, in some way, we could share the fun, the joy and the discipline of our lifestyle with them."

"That's an inspired idea," Pam enthused. "I do see what you mean, Valerie. The older generation have more time on their hands. Whilst children visiting the old folk in a home would bring cheer and energy to them, the old folk would be able to share time, life experience, and wisdom with the kids. How much more valid that would be when we're talking about an old yogis' home. I noticed when our grandchildren were tiny that Jimmy and I would spend hours playing silly games with them; hours that their loving parents simply did not have to spare, what with work and running the household."

"Yes," agreed Jamila, "I remember once spending an hour and a half climbing the bottom step of the stairs with my granddaughter! We had a little chant that we repeated: 'Up the step, and down the step, up the step, and down the step'. I was teaching her to climb stairs, but she didn't realise that. She was just having fun. It's the same with children's yoga classes. They're just having fun, but all the time they're absorbing tools and techniques to deal with life's challenges."

Susie had taught all age groups during her career, but she did firmly believe in introducing yoga to the young. Valerie had a very good point about their community finding a way of interacting with youngsters. Susie was determined to ponder this notion further.

"These questions are going well, Rob," she confided to her husband later. "I'm fascinated by them all, but I can't wait to hear Mum's query! She comes at it from a novel viewpoint. Her daughter teaches yoga. Her son-in-law and both grandsons practise yoga, and she lives in a yoga community. What will she ask, do you reckon?"

Rob laughed. "I think your mum's question will reflect the love and the commitment that you both share. It'll have a quirky aspect to it, I'm sure!"

CHAPTER 31

And Miles asked:

"When yoga originated in India, why does that country still have so many problems?"

Susie had to wait a little longer to hear her mother's question. The next one presented was from Miles. It was of a very serious nature, and Susie enjoyed relaying it to Yoga the following evening.

"India is a beautiful country," Yoga replied. "It contains the forests of my male predecessors and the seas of my female predecessors. India is as old as time itself. Those who choose to reincarnate in India do so with full knowledge of its difficulties. They come to address the extraordinary hardship and poverty. Hindus believe in karma and they grow up with an instinctive understanding about life and death. Yoga reinforces their cultural and religious beliefs. To return to Bernard's question, yoga *is* winning. Part of India's work here on the earth is to give yoga to the masses. Some years back, a well-known yoga teacher in America endeavoured to copyright certain yoga asanas. India responded swiftly and with great love. India copyrighted all yoga postures and then gave them to the world!" Susie smiled as she remembered this news item.

Yoga continued, "And then, to return to Jamila's question, masses of Indians practise yoga. Progress is being made, but there is still so much to be done. Dedicated folk are constantly trying to alleviate the diseases, the lack of safe drinking water, the utter poverty faced by many in India. These committed folk are endeavouring to bring education to remote areas; to change thinking about the 'untouchables' and about child marriage; to stop the sex trade, child abduction and the sale of children. India shows the extremes to the world. Perhaps the answer to Miles's question is to say that India's karma is to show the world the whole range of mankind's journey. Indians demonstrate the journey of the lotus flower. From the mud and the filth, the seed of the lotus flower is born; the stem travels up through the murky depths of mankind's lessons; then comes the blossoming of the most exquisite bloom and this is enlightenment. Perhaps India has to re-enact this process over and over again until all of mankind is saved."

Susie was moved to tears by Yoga's reply. She hoped that he had relayed it straight to Miles's mind. She did her best to repeat the answer to the class in just the way that it had been given. Many heads nodded wisely.

Rob was just as moved when she recounted the conversation to him later. He and Susie had loved visiting India. It was an experience of sensory bombardment. He would never forget the smells, the sounds, the colours, but most of all the smiles of the Indian people. Motorbikes were sold as a family vehicle and you would see the father driving with a child on his lap, the mother sitting side-saddle, wearing a sari, and holding a baby! One tuk-tuk driver had confided to them that, if he had a really good fare first thing in the morning, he would then take the rest of the day off and go home to play with his children. He didn't feel the pressure to make more and more money. It was enough to provide a reasonable living. His choice was to spend time with his family. Many fathers in the Western world could learn from that.

Of course, the poverty and the begging were heart-rending. Susie had given and given, and had been reduced to tears on a daily basis. But there were so many smiles, too. The parents were so proud of their children, who would be turned out in immaculate school uniform. The ladies wore their saris with such grace. Even the lowly job of watching over the shoes outside a temple was approached with conscientiousness. India gave the great gift of yoga to the world, and would remain the essential destination of all committed yoga teachers.

Susie was prompted to get out her photo albums from their Indian trips. They spent a nostalgic hour going through their memories with many a "Ooh, do you remember…?" or "Gosh, that was in…" Eventually, the precious albums were stowed back in the cupboard, but they felt an enduring affection and respect for all things Indian.

CHAPTER 32

And Maureen asked:

"Is Alice happy in Spirit World?"

Maureen's question was written in her small and neat hand. It expressed her somewhat tentative approach to life. She had always been a timid soul, and she was a little concerned that the others would think her query was a little odd.

Susie, however, smiled widely as she read out the question at the beginning of their evening practice. She offered the enquiry to Yoga during the long relaxation, and was delighted to hear his reply.

"Alice is very happy. She sends her love to you all. She is with Ted and she is drinking a virtual cup of tea. She raises her cup to you in a gesture of 'Cheers'. She says to tell you that she often spends time with Rosie, who is also happy. They look down lovingly on you all, but they're also busy and involved helping to heal and rehabilitate newcomers to Spirit World. Alice says to thank Maureen for her enquiry. She says that you are a special soul, Maureen, and that she sees the progress you have made. She's putting her hand on her heart and sending you her love." Susie received Yoga's reply with great joy, and she saw Maureen's eyes fill with tears as she relayed it to the class at the end of the practice.

Alice had been the first resident in Home from OM and was beloved by all. She and Susie had been next-door neighbours, but, more than that, they'd been soulmates. Alice and Ted bequeathed their cottage to create the home, and an eternal memorial to them was the meditation hut. It had been Ted's potting shed.

"What a beautiful question, Maureen," Susie said as she caught up with her walking out of the hall. "Thank you for asking that. I have a warm glow knowing that Alice looks down on us all, and that she observes your progress."

"I do, too," Maureen agreed. "I was a little concerned that you would all find my query a bit odd, but Alice meant so much to me. She kept a maternal eye on me when I first arrived. She showed me what unconditional love meant. You know that I didn't have a happy childhood, Susie, but Alice showed me that I could have a happy old age. She was such a special lady."

"She certainly was, and your question makes me feel that I've been with her for a short while," Susie smiled as her mother caught up with them.

"Wasn't that lovely to touch base with Alice," Marion enthused. "Thank you, Maureen. That was such a sweet thought."

Maureen looked shy but pleased.

"Alice and I spent such happy days together when Home from OM was being created," Marion continued. "We kept house for the others when all was in chaos here. Do you remember the day we sold my parents' house, Susie? You came home and we couldn't stop grinning!"

"I do remember that day," Susie smiled now as she saw the scene in her mind's eye. "It's taken a team of us to get this home for elderly yogis up and running. I'm so grateful to you and Alice, Mum. You both gave up your homes. But so much more than that, you gave love, time, energy and buckets of encouragement! You know, it's very easy to start taking everything for granted. In the beginning, having the home was a source of constant wonderment to me. But you know what they say: 'Familiarity breeds contempt'. The home's been in existence for so long that we've grown used to it. Thank you again, Maureen. Your question has really made me count my blessings. It's reminded me how eternally grateful I am to the wonderful people who made sacrifices to bring the home into being."

Susie's eyes were wet with tears when she gave first Maureen a big hug, and then Marion.

Over dinner there was more appreciation for Maureen's question. She began to feel like quite a celebrity! This experience had taught her something and she expressed this to Jean. "I've always been filled with trepidation," she confided. "When Susie first brought up this notion of asking a question, I was all of a dither. Then, from nowhere, came this idea. My heart jumped at the thought of enquiring after Alice. I remember Susie once saying that if a thought makes your heart sing, then it's the right thing to do; if a thought makes your heart sink, then it's definitely not the right thing to do. Well, I had to be a bit brave because it definitely made my heart sing!"

"I think you're braver than you believe," Jean said. "This was such a simple question, but so very beautiful. Well done, Maureen!"

The meal that the old yogis shared that night had a special quality to it. There was much talk about Alice. Reminiscence is important to us all, but perhaps it's essential to the elderly. After all, they've lived a long time. They have a lot of memories!

CHAPTER 33

And Jimmy asked:

"When I work with walking meditation, counting mantra on my hand, and when I engage the heart mudra, Hrdaya, I find that special place of peace within me. Why does it seem impossible for me to live there permanently?"

"My goodness," thought Susie, "these oldies of mine are coming up with some varied and fascinating questions!"

Even though the home had been in existence for almost fifteen years, the yoga life still had to be actively promoted on a daily basis. Human nature is such that constant repetition of wise messages is essential. Whilst the weekend was a time when the old folk could rest their bodies and allow the energies to settle, they still needed to return to the hall each Monday for fresh guidance.

Yoga responded to Jimmy's question in much the same way as Susie would have done. This is what he said: "Only a very few advanced gurus achieve the state of permanent samadhi. A lifetime's study of yoga still doesn't prevent the effect of worldly distractions. Repetition is essential. Coming back to your body, returning to your breath, reinstating that inner peace, these are all part of your practice. Yoga is not the sort of therapy where a student could be given a box of cures to take home. It's a way of life and it's all about the journey."

"I completely agree," Susie said, in her head. "Jimmy points out to us there that some practices work on him particularly well. Is that down to the student's nature, and the classical path that would most suit them as an individual?"

"That's definitely the case," Yoga said. "Interestingly, Jimmy quotes a doing activity, in the form of walking meditation, a doing activity in the form of counting mantra on the hand, and a doing and being activity in the form of Hrdaya Mudra. It seems that he is most suited to practices which involve his mind and his body. Finding a way of connecting them serves him well."

"Which classical path do you think Jimmy aspires to?" Susie asked.

"I would say that his inclination is towards hatha yoga, and that this leads him to raja yoga. Whilst this question is about enquiry, I don't see Jimmy as a gnana yogi."

"Yes, you're right. karma yoga and bhakti yoga don't quite fit him either. I will tell him what you've said at the end of the class." Susie glanced around her relaxed students. Jimmy was snoring gently.

All of the elderly yogis were interested in Yoga's reply to Jimmy. They all nodded at the fact that distraction was a problem for everyone. Susie watched them all and realised the massive difference between her oldies and other elderly people. They were completely engaged with life. These enquiries engrossed them. Whereas the majority of old people closed down and allowed their worlds to become smaller and smaller, the residents of Home from OM were growing and learning all the time.

Jimmy talked to the others on his table that evening, whilst they enjoyed their meal. "It fascinates me how some practices just click with me. Do you know what I discovered the other night? I was restless in bed. I just couldn't seem to get comfortable. It felt like all my limbs were awkward – I had too many arms! Pam was sleeping soundly and I really didn't want to disturb her, so I began to imagine counting mantra on my right hand. Instead of moving my thumb to the lowest joint of the little finger, I imagined doing it. Then I imagined moving to the middle joint of the little finger, and then the top joint, whilst reciting 'OM Mani Padme Hum' all the time. I followed the spiral, as we do in class, finishing up at the middle joint of the middle finger, and after just one round I felt more comfortable. I continued like that, from the top joint of the little finger across the top joints of the ring finger, middle finger, down the index finger and so on, all the time just using my imagination. At some point I drifted into a peaceful and relaxed sleep."

"Much like the one you enjoyed at the end of this evening's relaxation!" Pam said, twinkling at him.

"Actually, that's brilliant, Jimmy," declared Bernard. "I'm going to try that. It combines the mind with the body with the imagination beautifully. In fact, it opens up some ideas for working with people who are partially paralysed, who have perhaps had a stroke."

Jimmy looked astonished. Had he actually come up with something that had impressed Bernard?

Valerie joined in, enthusiastically, "Every question that has been presented to Yoga has provoked further discussion amongst us," she declared. "This has been such a successful initiative of Susie's."

"That's right, Valerie," Pam agreed. "What Jimmy's question brought up for me was to wonder which practices worked especially well for me. And my next thought was to admire yoga and yoga teachers for giving us such a wide variety of practices to choose from."

Valerie nodded. "I had a similar thought, Pam. I love chanting. It seems to work for me immediately. It's as though the act of singing allows me to move away from the everyday into a world of peace and serenity."

Bernard smiled at his wife. "I find that sequences have that effect on me," he said. "If I'm really out of my centre, I plump for Salute to the Sun, followed by Salute to the Moon. Three rounds of each and I'm right back on plan!"

This discussion continued on, long after the dessert of blackberry and apple crumble had been devoured. The next table to Bernard was similarly engaged. The folk here were comparing notes as to which movements and mudras were most effective for each of them. Maureen quietly confided that she loved visualisations. Julia spoke about the twenty-two part body relaxation. Miles found ujjayi breathing effective.

Susie, already down the road in her yoga centre, Wellness Within, would have been delighted to know that her old yogis were still engrossed with Jimmy's question. As she taught her evening group of students, whose ages ranged from eighteen to eighty, she wondered what questions they would be inclined to put to Yoga himself.

CHAPTER 34

And Pam asked:

"Do you tailor yoga differently for different nations?"

Pam's question followed her husband's. It took them from the personal to the general. Susie relayed the question to Yoga, following the procedure that they had established. She listened for the reply as her students deeply relaxed.

"This is yet another interesting question," Yoga began. "We've touched on the idea that each person has practices which work most effectively for them. We've also touched on the idea that each person has a different path of yoga which appeals to them. To an extent this is true for different nations. Indians grow up with knowledge of yoga. They may not come from a family who practise, yet they are surrounded by its impact. It's so entwined in their culture that it would be impossible to separate it. In hot countries, moving the body tends to be a pleasant outdoor pursuit. So, in Australia practising yoga on the beach is very popular. We can't imagine doing that on a cold, bleak January morning in Britain! Climate will inevitably bring about some differences, but the essential message of yoga is always the same."

"I think you're right to avoid the stereotyping of nationalities, Yoga," Susie countered, "but I'm guessing that different nations do have tendencies to look at the world through their own cultural lens. I heard once that Americans have very wide auras, which reflects the spaciousness of their country, whilst the Dutch have auras closer to them. They're more used to living in close proximity to their neighbours. I'm guessing that a country where there's a heavy emphasis on rules and regulations would readily embrace the discipline of yoga; while a country which tends to be more into free love and openness would readily embrace the heart-centred aspect of yoga."

"You make good points, Susie," Yoga agreed, "but the question was whether I tailor yoga differently to suit different nations, and to that I would have to say 'no'. The essence of yoga, the eternal message of yoga is the same for everyone. What differs, person to person, and nation to nation, is what aspect first attracts them to the practice. And what aspect engages them for the long-term."

"Yes, I completely get that. Different climates would show differences on a practical level, just like here we would open the windows in the summer and feel more expansive, then turn the heat up in the winter and seek more nourishing poses. The real difference, though, has more to do with inclination and openness than which nation you were born into." Susie thought for a moment about being British and what that meant to her. When she had studied History at school, she had sometimes been very ashamed to be British. However, she loved so much about British literature and architecture. She enjoyed living in England, but was she typically British? And had her nationality affected the way she approached her yoga? She thought not.

"Let's take another step here," Yoga continued. "This is really all about the choices that were made in Spirit World. When you set up this incarnation, Susie, you decided to be British. You had a mission to perform in this country. You are amongst the enlightened band who pledged to bring yoga to the West. You and your fellow yogis promised to make yoga mainstream. This you have achieved, I may add. You all chose to be yogis first and then looked at where you would be most effective."

"Ah, I see what you mean. This question is like asking: 'Do you tailor yoga differently to men and to women?' We chose our sex this time round for many complex reasons, and we may approach the practice slightly differently because of our choice, but that's down to relatively superficial inclinations. Yoga is always yoga." Susie brought the class back from their relaxation and relayed Yoga's explanation.

"I had a lovely conversation with Yoga tonight, Rob," Susie confided, as she tossed the salad.

"Is that guy still hanging around?" Rob teased.

"Yes, he's very much a fixture, I would say," she replied, grinning at him. "But it was about choosing this lifetime, and deciding which sex we needed to be, this time round, and which nationality. I'm really happy with my choices, how about you?"

"Oh yes," Rob agreed. "For all our faults and wrong decisions, I love being British. Nothing would induce me to part with my British passport. Having said that, though, I love other nations, too. I have huge appreciation for the Indians, a great affection for the French, tremendous admiration for the Dutch and the way they've combatted flooding in their country. The Germans are superb engineers, and I love Italian food, architecture and family values. I guess I would describe myself as a world citizen with a soft spot for England. As to whether I like being a man, that would be an affirmative! I love being your husband, Susie, and I've loved fathering our two boys."

"Do you feel that we've interacted with one another in previous lives, Rob?" Susie enquired.

Rob considered the question carefully. "Yes, I do. I felt that I knew you from the first moment that we met. It was, somehow, a deep knowing. A feeling of connection that was more than physical attraction, although that was there in buckets, too, of course!"

They caught eyes and laughed together for a moment. "I felt the same way," Susie confessed. "I fully accept the premise, though, that we may have been in a different relationship with one another previously. I might have been your father, or your daughter. We may have been close friends. Many people believe that we reincarnate in groups, so that we choose the same souls with whom to work out our lessons." Susie smiled at Rob, who was looking so handsome and bohemian at that moment. His long legs looked good in his jeans, and he was sporting a John Lennon T-shirt with the word 'Imagine' emblazoned across the front. His neat beard and longish hair only added to his masculine charm. Susie couldn't quite imagine him as a woman in that moment!

Back at the home, Jamila had been in a deep discussion with Pam and Jimmy about the current question. "Here I am, living in my adopted country," she said, "but I'm still Indian through and through. Yoga having originated in my country makes it feel like second nature to me. When I'm on my mat, though, I'm not aware of being Indian, or of living in Britain. I'm simply 'Self'. I'm spirit. Actually, I would say that I'm love."

"That's just lovely, Jamila," Pam replied. "I completely agree with you. I'm oblivious to superficial and external factors when I'm practising yoga. I just feel truly present and completely in touch with my inner being. I suppose my question wasn't really necessary, but, just out of interest, do you imagine Yoga himself to be Indian?"

Jamila laughed. "Yes, I do! That was a little bit tricky of you, Pam! But, I admit, rather clever. I do imagine Yoga to be Indian. What about you?"

"Yes, I see Yoga as being an Indian gentleman sitting on a cloud in the shape of a lotus flower," Pam replied. Jimmy laughed out loud at that image.

"That's brilliant, Pam," he chuckled. "I will never see him any other way!"

CHAPTER 35

And Elaine asked:

"Will Susie be an angel in Spirit World?"

Elaine had waited to hear other questions before she submitted hers.

Susie was a little embarrassed to relay this question to Yoga, but she did so during the long relaxation of the afternoon practice. She had a wry grin on her face as Yoga replied, "It doesn't quite work like that, but I'm going to answer the spirit of the question, rather than the question itself! Susie is already an angel because that is how many people perceive her. She has an angelic approach to sharing her love of yoga. Like an angel, she is caring, compassionate, and always ready to help. She has been a wonderful helpmate to me. Yes, I think we could describe her as an angel of yoga, or indeed a yoga goddess."

Susie blushed a little around the edges as she shared Yoga's reply with the group.

Elaine apologised. "I'm sorry to embarrass you, Susie, but I wanted my question to be more present and personal, if you know what I mean. I wanted it to be more like Maureen's. I love Yoga's reply, by the way!"

Marion piped up, "Susie's always been an angel to me! She was totally angelic as a baby, and she's continued to be angelic as she's grown into a woman. I will state emphatically that she's an angel of a daughter."

"Well, this angel brought Valerie into my life," Bernard added. "She clearly has heavenly gifts!" Bernard reached out to take his wife's hand. Her eyes misted over.

To everyone's surprise, Maureen jumped to her feet at this point. "Susie is already an angel!" She exclaimed adamantly. "She's transformed my ordinary, lonely little life into a state of bliss!" Maureen's friends were astonished to see this shy, retiring lady so fired up, and they broke into spontaneous applause!

Maureen sat back down on her mat with a thump. Her face looked more animated than they had ever seen before.

"All right," Susie laughed. "It's enough of all this. I shall be tempted to become a demon just to show you my other side. Or I could call in my husband. Rob could tell you some stories of a less angelic Susie!"

The assembled company moved off in their different directions. Marion was looking pensive. She caught up with Jean on her way into the dining room. "Jean, I'm having a little wonder about the fifteenth year anniversary of Home from OM. I'm sort of playing around with a notion of creating a poster for the yoga hall. Well, not so much a poster, actually, it would be more of a plaque. I'd like for us all to be part of designing it. It could be a list of yoga rules, and, after today, I fancy having a cartoon Susie-angel on the top. What do you think?"

Jean smiled. "Ooh, that's a lovely idea, Marion," she declared with enthusiasm. "I'm in. How about calling a meeting later in the sitting room? Shall I spread the word?"

The word was spread. The meeting was held. A lot of mirth accompanied the procedure, but a plan was hatched that evening.

Susie was oblivious to the secret scheme, but she too had been thinking about the anniversary. "Hi, Joanna, can you believe that the home has been going for fifteen years now?" Susie had phoned her friend for an informal chat.

"Wow, we must have been mere children, Susie, when it all kicked off!" Joanna chuckled.

"It'll be the anniversary on September 20th and I was wondering how best to mark it. Have a little think for me. See if you can come up with some good ideas." Susie and Joanna continued to chat for a while until Joanna's husband, Mark, arrived home from work.

"I must go, sweetheart," Joanna said, lightly. "One hungry husband has appeared. Have a great evening."

Susie woke early the next morning. She glanced at the clock and saw that it was 5.00am. The birds were singing outside, and Susie closed her eyes again to listen. A lively blackbird was leading the chorus, joined now and then with the familiar pigeon chant: 'Ricardo Pompidou, Ricardo Pompidou'. Susie smiled as she remembered the story that Alice's husband, Ted, had told her twins. He insisted that there was a very famous pigeon called Ricardo Pompidou. He was a brave pigeon who had countless adventures. He was so revered amongst the pigeon population that all pigeons were taught to chant his name each day.

Still amused, Susie slipped into that state between sleep and wakefulness. Suddenly a vision came into her mind's eye. It was a beautiful young woman. She was dressed in brightly coloured ethnic clothes – raiments somewhere between Native American Indian and Aztec. She was laughing. This was no angel, but very much a flesh-and-blood woman. Small children were gathered around her; some of them were clasping her hands, some were hanging from her skirts, and one little girl was wrapped around her leg. The children were all clamouring for her attention, but this young woman was looking straight at Susie and laughing. Her eyes were full of delight and mischief. Susie recognised a kindred soul. Her heart leapt, and she reflected the smile deep within her. The vision faded, but the memory of it remained. There was so much joy in that picture. Susie took it as a message. "Have fun," the woman seemed to be saying. "Look after your flock, but have fun too. Keep smiling. Be colourful. Spread joy."

CHAPTER 36

And Marion asked:

"We have so much fun here. Susie has told us that enlightenment does not have to be serious. My question is: 'Do you have fun in Spirit World? Is there laughter and merriment?'"

Eventually it was the turn of Susie's mother to ask her question. Susie had been very curious to know what it would be. It seemed coincidental that Marion's query would be on this subject, following her vision that morning, and Susie was delighted to relay it to Yoga.

The students relaxed deeply as Yoga gave his reply directly to Susie. "There is much merriment in Spirit World. Sometimes we, somewhat uncharitably, laugh at the goings-on on Earth! I would describe Spirit World as a more vivid version of life on Earth. We remember all the emotions, but life here is all about energy. So we remember the energy of laughter and fun. We remember and rejoice at the connection that comes with laughter. The lightness of amusement is very prevalent here. I would say that the air is filled with love, light and blessings. This we shower on you earthlings whenever there is an opportunity. And, yes, Susie's right. Enlightenment does not have to be serious!"

Susie smiled at Yoga's statement. Her mother was naturally a happy person, but she had never been as openly happy as she was here in Home from OM. It gladdened Susie's heart to know that her mum was having fun with all the old yogis.

"Laughter *is* just energy, isn't it Yoga?" Susie asked. "The longer we're all together in this yoga community, the lighter our energies become. Laughter energy is very light. Whenever I look at the Dalai Lama, I smile. He has such a twinkle in his eye. He seems to find fun wherever he goes."

"That's it exactly, Susie. You asked if there were great teachers who were sent as joy ambassadors to your planet. The ability to share mirth is a sign of a very enlightened soul. This is a soul vibrating at a high frequency."

Susie turned her mind back to her training as a yoga teacher. Her tutor had this ability to laugh at life and its vagaries. One of her colleagues on the diploma course had once stated that their tutor was 'full of unexpected laughter'.

The group were interested in Yoga's answer to Marion's question. Bernard smiled, knowingly. "I remember a time when I never laughed," he admitted. "I missed out on so much fun when my children were small. I took life so seriously, and I squashed any suggestion of jollity in my family and my employees."

Valerie looked at her husband with a gentle smile. "Yes, Bernard, but you see how you represent the truth of Yoga's reply. As you practised more and more yoga, your energies became lighter and lighter. I've seen you literally rolling around the floor with little Charlotte! Mind you, your granddaughter is enough to make anyone laugh. She's irrepressible! You're making up for lost time, darling."

Bernard squeezed his wife's hand.

Maureen spoke up, surprising her friends again with how forthright she was becoming. "I've laughed more since I've lived here than all of the rest of my life."

"I've literally watched you change, Maureen," Julia said. "You're living proof that living in a yoga community is healing. I feel now that you are realising who you really are. You're moving towards your full potential. You're a very special lady."

Maureen was very touched by this praise. "Yes," she thought, "I'm finally learning that life can be fun, even for me."

Susie walked to the dining room with her mother. "I love your question, Mum," she enthused. "It's so lovely to see how happy you are here. I recognise that Dad didn't bring out the funny side of you. When I look back to my childhood, it was always Dad and I that I remember laughing."

"That's true, Susie," Marion admitted. "I don't think I was ever truly myself while your dad was around. I was kind of the 'doer', the facilitator. I was in the background, setting everything up so that you and Jim could have a good time. I didn't actually feel resentful at the time. I was very close to my parents, of course, and they were always there for me. But since you created Home from OM laughter has become a daily activity. And since I moved in here hugging and laughing have become my bread and butter!"

That was the cue for Susie to give her mum a big hug. It was a hug that said, 'I'm sorry'. It was a hug that said, 'I love you'. It was a hug that said, 'Thank you for being you'.

There would be a great deal of laughter in Rob and Susie's house that weekend. Max and Megan had planned to come down for a visit and, on a whim, Toby came with his new girlfriend as well. Sophie was the vivacious brunette who Toby had met at his brother's wedding. Being Megan's cousin and knowing her so well meant that Sophie fitted beautifully into the foursome. The house was filled with the energy and laughter of young people. There was much teasing and a great deal of banter. The immediacy, the speed of their repartee was a joy to behold. Susie and Rob were gathered in immediately, and were treated with light-hearted respect.

During the evening, the wedding video was played with much glee.

"Look, look," Megan exclaimed. "That's the first moment that Toby spotted Sophie! I love it! He does an absolute double take!"

"Oh, come on Megan, you can't compare that with the moment that Max turns to watch you come up the aisle! He looks as though he's going to melt with love and pride!" Sophie smiled cheekily at her cousin.

"Okay, ladies, that's enough taking the rise out of the fellas," Max proclaimed. "But just look at our folks – they're still in love after for absolutely ever! We're bound to be soft!"

All eyes turned to Rob. "If I could have one wish for both my fine sons," he exclaimed, "it would be that they're as happy with their wives as I've been with mine. Love grows around Susie." His twinkling eyes told the full story, and the young people were touched.

It was great to have the house full of youngsters and Marion remarked on this fact when she came to lunch on Saturday. "It's so good to be around my grandsons, Susie. I feel as though they somehow suck us all into their youthful amusement. It's as though we're allowed to be honorary youngsters for a short while!"

"I know just what you mean, Mum," Susie agreed. "Do you think living with old folks means that you're cut off from young energy?"

"Not at all!" Marion exclaimed, "Sometimes we all act younger than them! I think being old is sometimes about going backwards. We can, as you know, become definitely giggly. But I see where you're coming from. It's a different energy and our lifestyle is slower, lazier. It's really refreshing that these four gorgeous young ones can come in occasionally and pep us up!"

Max, ever the more practical twin, spent some time in the garden of Home from OM. He did some weeding, working alongside Jamila and Elaine. "Rosie's garden looks just stunning," he enthused. "It was so worth all your hard work ladies." The ladies were pleased with this praise, and stood back to admire their planting with a fresh eye.

"The colours do work well, don't they?" Jamila replied. "We're going to have to keep a close eye on those perpetual geraniums, though. They're beautiful, so vivid a purple, but they spread like wild fire."

Toby meanwhile was using his artistic and creative skills to help Marion design the surprise plaque for his parents. "I love the idea of 'Yoga Rules'. It can be read two ways. That's clever, Gran," he said, with a grin.

"Now don't mention this to your folks, Toby," Marion warned. "We're keeping it close to our chests. Do you know anyone who can make it for us?"

"I can soon find someone," he promised. "Sophie and I'll do some research for you. I'll text you the details, but, when you're ready to action it, let me know."

The weekend passed all too quickly. It had become a tradition to all have Sunday lunch at the home when the twins visited. Joanna was delighted to provide a scrumptious meal for them all, and the old folk went up on the energy of the young. Marion had a good dose of laughter, and they were certainly all enlightened by some of the hilarious stories told by the young people!

CHAPTER 37

And Jean asked:

"What sort of world will our grandchildren inhabit?"

Susie was still in the afterglow of their lovely weekend, but she recognised that this question was a serious one and it meant a lot to Jean. She and her daughter, Lucinda, had fallen out. Jean, consequently, saw very little of her rowdy grandchildren.

Yoga replied in this way: "The next generation have difficult times to navigate. The world is facing some incredible challenges in the form of global warming, animal extinction, famine, and war. It's going to take innovative thinking and robust commitment to turn the planet around. One advantage that the next generation have in abundance is communication. The internet has opened up a whole new way of living. Young people come equipped to use the media to make great changes. And they're brave. Remember they've been born into this world. They're ready for the fight. I think that Jean's grandchildren and their generation will save the earth."

Susie relayed Yoga's response to the elderly yogis at the end of their practice. She added her own positivity by stating, "Seeing our sons and their partners this last weekend has convinced me that all will be well. These young people have positivity and energy for life which will see us through. When they bring children into the world, they'll bring with them the wisdom of the ages. I have such faith that 'all is well, and all shall be well.' However, I do see Jean's concern. We're all leaving them with some very difficult tasks to accomplish."

Jean sat by Jamila, Pam and Julia for dinner. They were all grandmothers. "Do you worry about the future for your young people, Jamila?" Jean asked.

"I used to," she replied, honestly. "I find that I don't any more. Yoga gives me my answers and I'm now much more open to trusting. I believe that we are in the hands of Brahman. If he wishes for our grandchildren to overcome the modern-day challenges of the world, they will do so."

Pam looked pensive. "I read once that we don't own the earth, we simply borrow it from our grandchildren. In some ways I really see Jean's underlying thought. We've not done a very good job of looking after the earth. Something else that I read is relevant: 'Man came; man saw; man broke things'. Our own impact on the earth right now is fairly mild. We're vegetarian so we're observing the rule of ahimsa and protecting the animals. We drive seldom, so we're reducing the pollution caused by vehicles. We don't fly, we don't use chemicals, and we actively support charities. But, in the past, we have all no doubt contributed to the problems on the planet."

Julia looked closely at Pam, "You're right, Pam, we're all guilty of trespasses against the planet, but I believe that Jamila is right, too. I love my grandchildren so much. They both have such inner strength. I see in Georgina and Lily our hope for the future. What we really need to leave them, in our wills, is love, laughter and courage. When you look at what our generation has overcome and achieved, it cheers you. All things are possible. I have to believe that we've done more good than harm."

Jean considered all these comments. "There must be a plan, mustn't there?" she mused. "It has to have been preordained. Yoga teaches us that there are forces greater than ourselves: angels, spirit guides, the archangels, the Masters – they're all better equipped than us to see the bigger picture. Yes, I feel reassured. The world that our grandchildren live in is the right world for them. They will work out their lessons with the skills with which they've been provided."

"That's right, Jean," Jamila agreed. "And they'll work out their lessons with the skills that we have given them, too."

"What a lovely way to look at it," Julia smiled. "And even though you don't see your grandchildren very much, Jean, they've still inherited from you through their genes."

"Life's complicated," Jean laughed suddenly. "It's sometimes all too big to get our heads around it! I'm going with the trust thing. I'm going to wrap my grandchildren in white light every time I think of them. I'm going to hold them in my heart, and I'm going to pray for them. There, that all feels much more positive! And yes, our grandchildren will inhabit the world which is right for them."

No-one can tell what the future will hold for their continuing family, but Susie was delighted to see how much discussion was stimulated by the questions that were posed to Yoga.

CHAPTER 38

And Julia asked:

"Do we need to teach children kindness and compassion?"

Julia had been a school teacher. She had been surprised sometimes at just how malicious her charges could be.

Susie relayed this question to Yoga in the long relaxation, as they had arranged.

"Interesting that this question follows the last one," Yoga began. "When souls are in Spirit World they're innocent. They're surrounded by unconditional love. They're filled with love, light and blessings. They choose with whom they wish to interact on Earth. If they choose to be born into a yoga family they will grow up observing kindness and compassion. But if they choose to be born into difficult and violent circumstances, kindness and compassion will be missing from their lives. We cannot intervene, in Spirit World, unless we receive a definitive request. Our hands are tied. All souls have free will, and they must work out their own karma. It's incumbent on teachers, leaders and parents to instruct children in kindness and compassion, but their biggest influence will always be their immediate circumstances."

Susie listened hard. "I remember when my little twins would squabble no end," she thought. "Seeing them at the weekend reminds me of how much love there is between them now. Those petty arguments were just that. They were superficial and unimportant."

"You did still endeavour to teach them goodness, though, Susie." Yoga remarked, hearing her thought.

"When you look around the world, Yoga, you notice that some people recover from a disadvantaged or abusive childhood, and some don't. Some folk join a yoga class in later life and make real strides in the healing department. Others sink under the weight of their burdens. This must come down again to their life plan. If yoga could intervene with everyone at an early age, would they all overcome their difficulties?"

"The younger the child who starts yoga practice, the more benefits they will receive. This is not in doubt. But yoga's not a one-size-fits-all pursuit. Some folk bring great resistance to healing from Spirit World. The best care in the world cannot cure without cooperation."

Julia nodded wisely as Susie relayed Yoga's comments. "Everyone needs to be reminded to be kind and compassionate," she commented, "not just children. And I do totally get that the earlier children begin to practise yoga, the better the life training will be, but, on some level, I'm still astonished that kindness does not come naturally. Why didn't God or Brahman programme it in?"

"That's a really good point," Valerie agreed. "I'm guessing that Bernard will raise the issue about balance in the world about now!"

"You took the words out of my mouth, Valerie," Bernard laughed. "There must always be a balance; a balance between good and bad, left and right and so on. The yin and yang symbol reminds us of this."

"I'm taking a detour here," Jean remarked, "but in my experience love has to be taught, too. Some children are easy to love, we would describe them as lovable, but others are not. My own daughter, Lucinda, was a challenge in every respect and she was definitely not lovable! Then there's degrees of love as well, isn't there? You might love a neighbour or a good friend, but that love will probably never be as strong as love for family. After all, we call them 'loved ones' don't we?"

"In a perfect world," Marion chipped in, "a child would be born to a loving family. That child would be gently encouraged to be kind and caring towards others. The child would be loved constantly, even if they were sometimes mischievous. The parental example would reinforce the message. The child would observe that their family all loved one another and were kind to each other. The thing is that the world's not perfect!"

"This is so true, Mum," Susie agreed. "I'm pretty convinced that's the point! We're here to find a way of dealing with our imperfections and the imperfections of others. If by teaching children kindness, compassion and love from an early age we can ensure that their coping skills are well developed, then they'll be better equipped to deal with all the imperfections."

The old folk went off to dinner with a great deal to discuss. Bernard's granddaughter, Charlotte, was mentioned often. She was the only little one who regularly visited the home, and she was a firm favourite with all.

Kitty Kara made her presence felt that evening in the sitting room. She sat first of all with Jean, and then took up residence on Miles's lap. He smoothed her fondly.

"Kara's a good example of our point here," Miles stated. "We treat her with kindness and love. She repays that affection and gives us love back. But animals that are badly treated learn to attack first. It's much harder to rehabilitate a rescue animal than to work with a kitten or puppy."

"I like that analogy, Miles," Julia agreed. "I find that I'm a little confused. It seems that the more questions that we ask, the more complicated everything becomes!"

"Okay," said Bernard, leaning forward and looking animated. "Are we all happy with the idea that we set up this incarnation in Spirit World? Suppose the main lesson we have to learn is compassion. Then we'll sit around the table with our spirit guides and advisors and we'll discuss how best to learn the lesson. If we create a family and a life where compassion is missing, we have to find a way of overcoming these circumstances. Our difficulties will so challenge us that we have to call in all our inner reserves and wisdom from past lives to find a way to compassion. Does that make any sense?"

The group nodded their heads.

"Now suppose our aim for this lifetime was to encourage others to be compassionate. Then we might choose to be born into a yoga home where love, kindness and compassion were already present in abundance. That would give us a solid foundation to take out into the world. We would have a springboard to launch our mission. Does that make sense?"

Again the heads nodded, but now Jamila intervened. "Explain to them, Bernard, why we don't remember our mission once we're born," she said.

"Ah, that's a good point, Jamila," Bernard said. "Now suppose that you had set up a lifetime to learn about desertion. Suppose you had left your wife and six children, in a previous lifetime, and simply abandoned them. Now you want to experience that desertion so that you can learn from it, so you and your advisors set that up in this present incarnation. But if you held on to the knowledge of your mission after being born to this life, you would be constantly looking at your watch and speculating, 'I wonder when he's going to leave?' You see, in order for the lesson to be valid, it needs to have impact. We have to fully experience the emotions of abandonment."

"Ah, I get it," Julia piped up. "Our lessons unfold gradually. So we could say that children who resist being loving and kind are learning a lesson. They will eventually, hopefully, discover that folk respond very differently to them when they acquire the attributes of compassion and kindness."

"Yes," Bernard agreed, "and certainly yoga being taught in schools would give them a helping hand."

This discussion continued on until the old yogis gradually drifted off to bed. Kitty Kara had enjoyed the company and was reluctant to leave Miles's lap. He stayed on for a while, enjoying the peace of the sitting room and reflecting on the evening's conversation. His mind turned back to the day that he met his partner, Marco. It was a revelation to Miles to meet anyone with such a lot of love on offer. Marco's heart was wide open. He seemed to embrace the whole world, and to spread love wherever he went. Miles had been brought up with kind parents, but there was a very English reserve to their affection. Consequently, Miles was bowled over by Marco's exuberance.

Miles began to consider the different qualities of love. He'd never had children, but his life had been filled with affection. "I wonder if that was one of my lessons to learn this time around," he mused. "Did I come to learn that there are many different types of love, and there's also love itself. Here in the home we live in a state of perpetual, not necessarily particular, love." At that moment, Kitty Kara stood up and had a wonderful stretch. Then she jumped off Miles's lap and made for the kitchen for a late night snack. Miles smiled and headed upstairs to bed.

CHAPTER 39

And Valerie asked:

"We all fully support the idea that yoga should be taught to everyone: the young, the adults, the elderly. Do you think of moulding people, Yoga? Do you see us as pieces of clay with which you can create incredible works of art?"

Susie smiled at this question. Valerie was a very smart lady with impeccable taste. You could see this in the way that she dressed, and in the way she kept the bedroom which she shared with Bernard. Valerie had been a buyer for a top-notch department store. She had an eye for colour and style.

Yoga replied to the query in this way: "If only it were that simple! Everyone comes to Earth with a mission and a lesson, or lessons, to learn. They also arrive with potential for growth. They are capable of reaching their fullest potential, but there are no guarantees. During the complications of life on this planet, it's highly possible to become sidetracked from your life's mission. Many people are diverted from their purpose and return to Spirit World somewhat disappointed. When they look back over their last life-time they can readily observe the opportunities that were missed, and they can see where lessons were repeated over and over again. If all people learnt the lesson the first time it was presented to them, it would save a lot of time! Certainly, some folk provide us with good material. If they're open to receiving guidance, and if they're willing to ask for help, then some moulding can take place. It's important to bear in mind that help must always be requested. All souls have free will, so we can't intervene unless asked."

"I do feel that my life has been shaped, Yoga," Susie remarked. "By practising and teaching yoga for so many years, I've absorbed the eternal truth. This shapes my every decision. I must also admit that these questions have moulded my outlook on life."

"That's correct, Susie. You're one of those people who works with me. You ask for help; you ask for answers; you learn your lessons. Your old yogis, too, are really open. They're listening to inner guidance. They've been excellent clay!"

"How do I explain your answer clearly to Valerie, Yoga? Please give me a simple sound bite." Susie looked expectant.

"I don't seek to mould anyone into the shape that pleases *my* eye. The truth is that life, and the inner essence of each soul, produces the finished work of art."

"That's perfect. Thank you, Yoga." Susie relayed this response to her group.

"All the way through the relaxation I kept getting distracted by the notion that I was being manipulated into better order," Pam laughed.

"I couldn't get past the image of us all standing on a shelf," Jimmy admitted. "There we were, painted and perfect, quite ready to be sold!"

Valerie grinned at her fellow students. "Now, now, this was quite a serious question," she defended herself. "Life itself obviously brings about quite a lot of change and moulding. We're bound to be altered by the people we meet and the experiences we have. I was just curious to know how much of a part Yoga plays in all that."

Bernard jumped in here to support his lovely wife. "It was a good question, Valerie. Take no notice of their teasing. I would guess that it's directly down to how much you're prepared to take Yoga into your life. A guru, for instance, who has totally embraced every aspect of yoga, would be utterly shaped by the discipline. Someone who attended one class per week, however, would have plenty of other influences to pull them out of shape."

Susie smiled at them all. "The fact is," she reminded them, "that none of us are perfect. If we had been, we wouldn't have needed to return for the lessons of this lifetime. There will always be slight cracks and lumpy bits in our clay."

While Susie returned home and prepared for her evening class in Wellness Within, Marion spread the word that they needed a meeting in the sitting room after supper. They needed to discuss the wording for the 'Yoga Rules' plaque.

"Toby has undertaken to find the right artisan to produce this masterpiece," she began. "Now we have to mould the wording!"

Maureen volunteered to be the scribe, and the suggestions came in, thick and fast.

"Yoga seeks balance," offered Jamila.

"Yoga is a discipline," Bernard suggested.

"Yoga promotes health and well-being," Julia chipped in.

"Yoga works with the entire being." This was Pam's contribution.

"Yoga is for everybody," said Jean, who added, "but it's especially for us oldies!"

"Hold your horses everyone," Marion laughed. "Let's talk about format. There's a sort of 'Yoga is...' list that's emerging. We could do that down the centre of the plaque, if you'd like to. Toby suggested that we could vary the writing style. We could have some statements in italics, for instance; we could have some in script; and we could have some in bold."

"This is a lovely project," Valerie said, beaming. "What colour shall we have the background?"

As can be well imagined, the discussion was lively and productive. Maureen's hand ached at the end of the evening from writing down all the suggestions. She now volunteered to put them into some sort of order on her laptop and to email the finished product to Toby.

The future recipients of this gift, meanwhile, were completely oblivious to its planning. Susie's evening class being over, she had locked up Wellness Within and had gone home to share a chamomile tea with her husband.

"What was the question of the day, Susie?" he asked.

"Now, are you genuinely interested or are you just being kind?" she queried.

"Oh I'm genuinely interested," he retorted. "How can you doubt it? Besides, I'm pretty sure that this is the last one!"

"Now that's sneaky," Susie laughed. "You've been counting! I'm sorry if I've been a bore. I must admit I've been totally engrossed in all these enquiries. Today was Valerie's turn. She asked Yoga if he moulded us like clay. It brought about some amusement from the others with Jimmy picturing a row of finished yogis on a shelf, all painted and perfect! But it stimulated some good debate, I can tell you. Yoga explained that we have to be willing to ask for help and guidance, and that we have to be open to our lessons, then it's possible for us to be shaped. He emphasised, though, that he doesn't shape us into his idea of perfection, but that each individual is shaped by his chosen path. It's fascinating stuff."

"It makes you reflect on how we've been shaped since creating Home from OM, and how the home has been shaped by its occupants," Rob replied, more serious now.

"That's true," Susie said. "The fabric, or clay, of the home was provided by Alice and Ted bequeathing their home; by my mum and my dad making financial contributions to both Home from OM and Wellness Within; by your dad giving his time and expertise to creating the meditation hut; and by the residents themselves. It's come into being over time. I guess you could say it's evolved much like a creative project. I'm sure potters begin with an idea of what they're going to make, but then the article develops an energy of its own."

"Mm, I know you've said that about your yoga classes too, Susie. You plan it, but sometimes the energy in the room and maybe a question that's voiced causes you to change direction. The practice, as you said, develops an energy of its own."

"That's it precisely," Susie agreed.

"But the spiritual clay is definitely love," Rob continued. "The home was born of love, and it runs on love. I have a question for you, Mrs Yoga Teacher," Rob laughed. "Do you think that prana and love are the same commodity?"

"Yes I do," Susie replied quickly. "Love in action is truly life force, life-giving energy. I once had a student who totally absorbed herself in yoga practice. She was a complete fan and it turned her life around. Her mother was in her eighties, but my student was such an advocate of yoga that she talked her aged mum into joining a class. Bless her, she had a bit of trouble at first getting up and down on the mat, having done little formal exercise before, but she enjoyed her first class. My student told me later that she had asked her mum after the class, 'So what was that all about, Mum?' And she replied, 'That was all about love.' Isn't that special? She got it in just one class."

"It comes back to intention, doesn't it?" Rob said. "Your intention is to spread the message of yoga through the medium of love. Remember I said to the boys and their ladies the other day, 'Susie grows love.' You really do. You sow love seeds wherever you go!"

"Ah, but that only works when I have fertile soil to work with," Susie grinned. "That's what you provide, Rob. You give me the means to express my love. We're like two oxen, yoked and ploughing together!"

"Now, that's a great picture," Rob chuckled, "but it brings us back to yoga again. The word yoga means to yoke, doesn't it? And as we plough, we unearth some good pieces of clay for Yoga to shape."

Susie reflected on this initiative of asking questions, as she cuddled into her husband in bed that night. It had been useful, there was no doubt about that. The oldies had totally embraced the idea. "Well, Yoga," Susie said to her mentor and guide, "I'm asking. Feel free to give me new ideas and to mould me as you wish."

CHAPTER 40

And Yoga concluded:

"Do good, every time you can, every way you can, to everyone you can."

Susie had taken a long walk that Saturday morning. She made for her favourite heath. As she passed through a narrow path, she brushed past the bright yellow flowers of gorse. The smell of the coconut-scented blooms filled the air. It transported her back to Kerala, Southern India. She remembered how vivid everything was there – the colours, the smells, and the cacophony of noise. Susie counted her blessings as she walked. She'd always been a worker, but she'd had a good life. She was surrounded by love, and had managed to juggle a happy family life with an equally happy and fulfilling career. She felt blessed.

Susie found a log and sat down to absorb the peace of the heath. Her hands made their way into the grounding mudra, where the thumb connects with the ring finger. She felt truly connected to the earth. Susie closed her eyes, and Yoga began to talk to her. "Yoga practice is based on enquiry, Susie. You and your elderly residents have embraced the inner essence of this ancient wisdom. From the first moment that we lie down on our mats, we enquire. 'Can I feel the ground beneath me?' 'How does my body feel today?' 'Am I in balance?' 'Is my mind truly present?' 'Can I connect with my breath?' In yoga, we live the questions."

"I see that, Yoga," Susie replied. "And you've shown me how we must also ask for help. When I talk to you like this, am I talking to my inner guru, or are you my spirit guide?"

"I am one and the same," Yoga replied. "There is *Brahman*, the Supreme Being, and there is *Atman*, the divine spark within each person. We are all one. Yoga means union."

"This moment is bliss, Yoga," Susie said. "I'm at one with you, I'm at one with me, and I'm at one with all that is."

When our questions are answered, there is a time of peace. But later more questions arise. There are more enquiries. It was several weeks later when an occurrence caused Susie to exclaim, "Yoga, why are people not straightforward? Why do they resort to deception and half-truths?"

The frustration behind the question came from dealing with a handyman that they'd employed to do a small job at the home. This guy constantly let them down. He would make an appointment and then not turn up. He always had a glib excuse, but he was just plain unreliable. Susie and Rob had been open to believing him at the beginning. They wanted to give him some work as he seemed down on his luck. Eventually, they had to sack him and endeavour to find someone else to finish his partially begun task.

Yoga saw an opportunity to explain a deep truth to his protégée. "Sometimes the image that someone presents to the world is very different from that person's self-image. It's like there's a lens in front of them. This lens distorts, so that the picture that the spectator sees is false. Let's take your elderly yogis as an example. Bernard is straightforward. He can be brusque, but he has an open channel to the world. What you see is what you get. Jimmy, though, is more complex. He presents a certain image to the world which is only partially correct. His own self-image is of a less confident, more needy person. People don't immediately see that because it's obscured by the lens. Miles – now, he's an enigma. He's really honest. He's filled with integrity, but what do you really know about him? Does he disclose his inner struggles? He's open and closed, all at the same time. Let's look at the ladies now. Jamila is all about love, but she tends to put herself at the back of the queue. She will give and give and give. She's filled with compassion for others, but she's reluctant to give it to herself. Eventually, someone like that will be giving an inferior gift, because they've exhausted their inner core. They've neglected to replenish themselves. Jamila's now aware of this tendency, since moving into Home from OM, by the way."

"I see what you mean, Yoga," Susie agreed. "So George, our handyman, presents an image to the world, and his lens is completely obscuring what lies within."

"That's right, Susie. He thinks that he's fooling everyone. Each time he's caught out in a lie he attempts to distract you with a more dramatic hard-luck story. It's become second nature to him now, so he barely knows that he's doing it."

"You have to feel sorry for someone who is so out of touch with honesty, don't you, Yoga?" Susie reflected. "It brings us back to our yoga rule of non-lying. I've reached the point where I don't believe a word he says, so I can't trust him ever again."

"I must remind you here, though, that there's a lesson for you as well. The frustration and distrust that you feel has pulled you away from your centre. Send him love and let him go."

Susie grinned. She'd been caught out and, yet again, Yoga was showing her the way.

"Let's continue with the lens over the inner self-image discussion, Yoga. And, no, I'm not trying to distract you! I'm going to let George go, I promise, but I'm really interested in the distortion, too."

"Shall we continue through the ladies in the home, then? Jean chose a rocky road. She's been pretty bruised along the way. She used to cover her feelings and put out an image of someone capable and 'in charge'. This was far from the truth. Letting her daughter go gave Jean permission to be her true self. The lens or filter has been removed. Now, Valerie presents a certain image to the world, but actually it's the same as her self-image. She really is a neat and fastidious lady. You'll have your own thoughts about quiet Maureen, but Alice was right when she sent that message from Spirit World. Maureen has made great strides." Yoga allowed his words to sink in.

"What about my lovely mum?" Susie enquired.

"Marion is a good case study, Susie," Yoga replied. "The person that Valerie sees, as Marion's friend, will be different from the person that you see, as her daughter. Both images are valid. The fact is that human beings are like crystals. You have many facets. You show different aspects of yourself to the different people with whom you interface."

"So how is that different from the lens that covers the inner self?" Susie challenged.

"Each facet of the crystal is projecting a different aspect of the true self. There's nothing false about that. It's not done on a conscious level and it's not done to deceive. You could look at the projections from the different sides of the crystal as being moods, or, indeed, the different colours in the rainbow."

"So the inner being is still true," Susie mused. "I get it now. So, let me see if I can get this right. Pam has no lens in place. She's like Bernard, what you see is what you get. And our newbie, Elaine, is pretty straightforward, too. Joanna sometimes shows me her shadow side, but she's open to learning all the lessons that come along. Jane's a little trickier, simply because I don't know her so well. I'm inclined to think that Jane is like a stick of rock, efficient all the way through! Then there's the last of our old yogis, our Julia. She loves, lives, learns, and then loves some more. Julia's beautiful on the outside and on the inside. How did I do?"

"The fact is that you make these judgements unconsciously, Susie," Yoga commented. "You pick up a lot of information from people's auras. Most of the time you're pretty intuitive, but then George came along to teach you a lesson! He pulled you away from your centre, or, to be more correct, you allowed him to disturb your equilibrium."

Susie laughed. "There's no escaping the lessons, Yoga! Thanks for putting me straight today!"

"You'll always get there in the end, Susie, with or without me. Remember to live by this saying: 'Do good every time you can, every way you can, to everyone you can.' Then you can't go wrong."

Susie felt lighter as she walked home.

There was a buzz in the atmosphere of Home from OM later that day. Secret plans were afoot. Maureen had emailed the details of the plaque off to Toby and he'd found an excellent guy to create it. Marion had received it in the post that morning, and had been sneakily taking it around to show her fellow yogis. They were all really pleased. "We're in good time," Marion said to Valerie, "but now we need to organise a card and the occasion."

"Leave the card to me," Valerie volunteered. "Bernard and I have been practising. We're rather good at making these computer cards. We'd love to put something together."

"That's excellent, Valerie. Thank you. Now I shall draw Joanna into our surprise. September 20th will be a splendid celebration for Susie and Rob." Marion busied herself to the kitchen. She was thoroughly enjoying all this subterfuge!

As expected, Joanna and Jane completely embraced the idea of celebrating the fifteenth anniversary of Home from OM. They discussed what sort of event Marion had in mind, and it was agreed they would offer afternoon tea. This always suited the elderly residents, and if the weather was clement, it could be held in the garden.

"Let's get some other yoga teachers involved," Joanna suggested. "I'll contact Elly, who offers laughter yoga, and Mark. Do you remember when he did that marvellous chanting afternoon? I'm sure they'll be keen to come and to bring some of their students."

"Good idea," Marion agreed, "and Toby, Sophie, Max and Megan are all up for it. How about the therapists who are so supportive of us all? The ones who work from Wellness Within have been really caring. Most of them offer a small reduction to the residents of the home. What do you think?"

"That would be excellent, Marion, but we'd better draw the line there. Jane and I are going to have to find sneaky ways of doing the catering as it is!"

The next week passed quickly. It was drizzling on the morning of September 20th but, never daunted, the yogis took the beautifully wrapped plaque, and the uniquely designed card into the sitting room. "We'll have to set up in here," Marion said to Joanna, making a sad face.

"It'll be fine, Marion," Joanna reassured her. "The forecast says that it's going to clear up at lunchtime. If that turns out to be the case, we'll lug everything outside. We've enough hands to make it light work. May I see the card that Bernard and Valerie created?"

"Of course you may, and I'd like you to sign it with clever words, too."

The card sported the words 'Keep calm and carry OM' on the front. Joanna expressed her approval and wrote: "To our beloved leaders on this special day! All my love, Joanna."

Susie and Rob had talked about the anniversary, but coming, as it did, hot on the heels of the wedding, they decided to keep it low key. They planned to pop down to the home after the residents had eaten their dinner, and to have a quiet drink with them. They were very surprised, therefore, to see Toby's car arrive in the drive. They'd been sitting and chatting after lunch, still completely oblivious of the events unfolding up the road.

The car doors opened and out came Toby, Sophie, Max and Megan. The girls looked particularly beautiful, both boasting light tans and pretty summer dresses. They were obviously in high spirits, and burst through the front door with cheerful shouts of "Anyone home?"

Rob and Susie leapt to their feet, laughing. "Yes, we're home. To what do we owe this pleasure? Did we forget that you were coming?" Rob looked quizzical.

"Oh, it was just a whim, Dad," Max fibbed. "The weather started to look up and we thought 'Let's go and shake up the old folks of the family!'"

"And Sophie and I have been shopping this week in the sales, Susie. We saw this and we both agreed that it's totally you. Do try it on. Please do, pretty please!" Megan gently urged her mother-in-law towards the stairs.

"What now?" Susie asked, looking completely bewildered. She hadn't planned on changing out of her cropped trousers anytime soon.

"Yes, right now," Megan insisted. "We can't wait to see you in it."

Susie decided to surrender to the gleeful pressure being exerted on her. The girls had chosen the prettiest dress. It was lilac, one of her favourite colours, and it had a most flattering cowl neckline. Susie, entering into the fun of the event, teamed it with some pretty high-heeled sandals and some lilac drop earrings.

"Wow!" said Toby, as his mother swept down the stairs. "You're not bad for your age, Mum!"

"Thank you kindly," Susie replied tartly, "but now I'm all dressed up and nowhere to go."

"I know," Max said, lightly, "let's go up the road to Home from OM and surprise Gran. Toby and I have been arguing about which one of us is her favourite grandson. This is an important issue and needs to be resolved immediately!"

"This is true," Sophie agreed, grinning. "Good job Susie has a new dress for this occasion."

Still somewhat bewildered, Rob and Susie allowed themselves to be ushered up the road. They were intrigued to hear laughter coming from the back of the building. Guiding them in through the front door, and then down the hall to the sitting room, Toby continued to distract them with lively conversation. As they stepped through the French doors to the garden, the full impact of the glorious scene stunned them both. Tables had been set up, resplendent with cakes, scones, sandwiches and all manner of small delicacies. There was a huge banner proclaiming 'Happy 15th birthday, Home from OM!' The garden was full of their friends, who, as one voice, yelled "Surprise!"

Rob was first to collect his wits, and to exclaim, "This is fantastic! Whose wonderful idea was this?"

Max took his grandmother by the shoulders and gently pushed her forward. "Who else but Gran would have pulled this together!" He exclaimed, proudly.

"Well, it may have been my idea initially," she said, quickly, "but it's definitely been a team venture."

Susie roused herself from her shock and gave her mother a big hug. "This is the best surprise ever," she stuttered. "Thank you all so much! I'm completely overwhelmed."

Susie's face beamed with delight, and Joanna caught the moment with her camera.

"One more surprise, Susie," her mother exclaimed, "and then we'll let you circulate and have fun."

With that, Marion handed the gift to Susie and the card to Rob. A hush settled on the company as Susie tore off the paper. The plaque was amazing. All the discussion had proved to be worthwhile, and Toby's contact had produced a masterpiece. Susie gasped and leant against Rob. "This is utterly exquisite," she said, breathlessly. "I'm speechless."

Rob opened the carefully created card and found it to be signed by all the residents of Home from OM, and all those present there today. "Well, that's a keeper," he said immediately. "Thank you so very much. My wife and I would like to express our heartfelt gratitude to you all."

Rob grinned at his son. The 'my wife and I' wording had not escaped Max. It had not been so very long before that he had uttered those very words in the garden at his wedding.

Susie propped up the plaque on one of the tables. It was much admired. "Do notice the figure on the top, Susie," Elaine teased her. "It's a Susie angel!"

Susie laughed. "I'm loving the words. You've all given such careful thought to this. It'll look fantastic in the yoga hall."

Bernard joined them at this moment. "We wanted to get the words just right, Susie," he exclaimed, putting his arm around her shoulder and giving her a squeeze. "They have to be read in your voice, though, to have full impact."

"You see you haven't lived in vain, Susie," Valerie stated. "We have been listening!"

The plaque would find itself taking pride of place in the yoga hall the very next day. That afternoon, though, was all about celebration. Mark had brought along some lively Bollywood music, and the sound of the chatter and laughter could be heard throughout the 'yoga village'. Food was eaten, fun was had, folk were hugged. Truly a good time was had by all.

Susie caught up with Megan and Sophie. "Girls," she enthused, "thank you so much for my lovely dress. How very sweet, and how rather sneaky you are! I had no suspicion at all! But I'm so glad I didn't turn up here looking scruffy. That was really thoughtful of you both." Susie caught them both up in a group hug. Her heart was full of love for the two ladies that her boys had chosen as their own.

One of the high points of the occasion was when Rob and Susie found themselves talking to Elly and her husband, Richard. Elly's face was alight with joy when she confided in them, "We're going to open an old yogis' home! We're so excited. We've found just the right premises, and our offer on it has been accepted. Please can we pick your brains? We'd so appreciate your input."

Susie and Rob hugged their friends warmly. "That's the best news ever," Susie enthused. "Of course we'll help in any way that we can."

It was much later that night, when they fell exhausted into bed that Susie thought, "I'm truly blessed. I have the best job in the world, and I'm surrounded by love. Home from OM, you have been my life's mission, my destiny. Long may you continue. And we have the beginning of an epidemic! Another old yogis' home is about to be born."

Susie fell asleep, gently humming a Bollywood song.

YOGA RULES
Yoga is:

Namaste	Eternal	*OmShanti*
Breathe	Loving	**Be Still**
Balance	Kind	Enquire
Be Present	Blissful	*Be Kind*
Love	Disciplined	**Joy**
Savasana	Liberating	Mudras
Well-Being	Mindful	*Harmony*
Relax	Ageless	**Chant**
Prana	Health-promoting	Ahimsa
Be aware	A way of life	*Meditate*
	Unity	

- Home from OM - Home from OM - Home from OM - Home from OM - Home from OM -

THE

END

ॐ

Made in the USA
Columbia, SC
08 July 2017